The Save Five Club

one woman's quest to help animals

By Janet Vormittag

The Save Five Club

By Janet Vormittag

First Edition 2020
Second Edition 2023

ISBN: 978-0-9986987-1-7

Published by:
JLV Enterprises LLC
Cats and Dogs

www.JanetVormittag.com

Printed in the U.S.A.

Dedicated to Wendy Sue Wamser

March 14, 1949 – May 31, 2019

My friend Wendy Wamser was diagnosed with Stage IV cancer in December 2018. I asked her what was on her bucket list, expecting her to say she wanted to visit her daughter who lived in Florida. To my surprise, travel wasn't what she desired; what she wanted was to read the next book in my "Save Five Series," a book that was only percolating in my head.

"How much time do I have?" I asked.

"I don't know," she said with a frankness that was her hallmark.

I started writing, but six months wasn't long enough for me to write a book or say goodbye to a friend of more than 30 years.

Thanks to Kristina VanOss, Pat Pritchard and Gayle Thompson for helping make this book a reality.

Other Books by Janet Vormittag

Dog 281 (1st book in The Save Five Series)

More Than A Number (2nd book in The Save Five Series)

You Might Be a Crazy Cat Lady if...

You Might Be a Crazy Cat Lady if... (Vol.2)

Cat Women of West Michigan, the Secret World of Cat Rescue

A Fox in Church

I remember
the fox at church
curled around the woman
who sat two pews ahead.
That ravenous fox
chewing its own tail
or was it a leg, a foot,
its mouth stuffed full of fur
silent, chewing.

I sat in rapt attention
the little girl with steady focus
who stared down those
black, beady eyes
of the once quick brown fox
now coiled on the shoulder
of Mrs. Baxter, her gray curls
catching on his snout.

I never heard a word of the sermon.

~ Gloria Klinger

Chapter 1

It's funny how you can live life in a cocoon, oblivious to what is happening around you. Then there's an awakening. The blinders come off. What was once invisible is everywhere.

My awakening started with a telephone call while working at an animal shelter in Northern Michigan. A hiker found an injured beagle while hiking the North Country Trail in the Manistee National Forest. The dog's leg was caught in a trap. The guy—his name was Dale—didn't know what to do, so he called the county animal shelter.

Knowing the national forest covered a lot of acreage, I asked Dale if he could show me the location of the animal. I arranged to meet him in an hour where the trail intersected Koenig Road. I called Jason Bentley, our animal control officer.

"Hey, Jason, you available?"

"Could be, Alison, but what are you getting me into this time?" Jason and I have history, maybe more aptly called baggage.

"A guy found a dog with his leg caught in a trap. Sounds like more than I can handle alone."

"Absolutely I can help. When?"

"I told the guy that we'd meet him in an hour. He's way up in the northeast corner of the county. Can you pick me up?"

"Sure. Give me a half hour."

I'm relieved Jason and I are on friendly terms. After sneaking behind his back and going undercover to a dog fight, I worried our friendship had been damaged beyond repair. Thankfully, he got over his anger, but what remained was a strained relationship. However, I had every intention of proving myself worthy of his trust again.

I thought I'd lose my job over the incident, too. The only reason I didn't was because Sheriff Marc VanBergen had been a player. I'm still shocked that he found enjoyment watching two dogs tear each other apart. His involvement in the so-called *sport* was why he hindered investigation of dog fighting in the county. Unfortunately, the sheriff was shot and killed when the fight organizer realized he had helped me escape. VanBergen had been Jason's boss. I suspect Jason blamed me for his death. Facts can't be disputed. The blame was partially mine, but my finger didn't pull the trigger. I wasn't the one blackmailed into obstructing justice.

So, Jason and I continued to work together. Maybe someday we'd overcome my misstep and truly be friends again. Until then, I was thankful he took my calls and was willing to help when I needed assistance. And today was one of those days.

Silence accompanied us on the ride to the far corner of the county. The only words between us were for directions on where we were going.

"He said he'd meet us where the trail crosses Koenig Road."

Jason knew the area. When we reached the trail, there wasn't anyone around. Jason tooted the horn.

"Let's head north. He said it was north of the road," I advised.

Jason grabbed a pair of leather gloves, a muzzle, a collar and lead and a blanket. "If we need a carrier, we'll come back," he said,

Just as we were about to head out, a young man came walking toward us from the trail.

"Dale?" I asked him.

"That's me."

"I'm Alison. This is Jason."

"He's about a mile from here. I heard him barking, and he sounded stressed. I love dogs, so I had to check it out," Dale told us.

"Could you get close to him?" Jason asked.

"He let me pet him, but his leg looked bad. The trap is caught between two trees. Looked like he'd been dragging it around. I didn't dare mess with it. Didn't want to get bit."

"Do you think he'll be able to walk or will we have to carry him out?"

"I don't know."

We decided to take the carrier. It would be a safer way to transport the dog if he couldn't walk.

In typical beagle fashion, the dog started howling when he heard us coming. As soon as he came into view, I started taking photos with my cellphone. Everything needed to be documented. The dog wore a collar, which gave me hope of easily finding his owner.

After assessing the situation, Jason suggested muzzling the dog and covering its head with a blanket before trying to remove the trap.

"His foot looks bad. I think we need to get the trap off and get him to a vet ASAP," he said. "It smells bad too. Must be infected."

"Let's do it," I agreed.

The dog didn't fight having the muzzle put over his face or being covered with the blanket. He had enough sense to know we were helping. Once he was secured, I checked the collar, but there weren't any tags, just a plain leather collar with no identifying marks.

Dale and I held the shaking pooch as Jason freed the trap from the trees so he could have space to work. Once in the open, he was able to open the metal jaws that gripped the dog's leg. The dog yelped but didn't try to escape. I had worried the injury would bleed when the trap was removed, but it didn't.

"He must have been caught in there for a few days," I commented. The dog didn't want to go in the carrier.

"I'll carry him," Jason said.

"You sure? It's a distance."

"I'm sure. He's been traumatized enough. If he doesn't want to go in, I'm not going to force him."

Before we headed out, Jason pointed out the tag on the trap. It had a name—Joe DeYoung—and an address. "By law, trappers have to have their name on their traps," Jason said.

"Is it legal to trap in the state forest?"

"It is, but the trap is supposed to be staked down. Apparently, it wasn't. It was probably set for coyote."

I picked up the rusted trap and turned it over in my hands. Dried blood with bits of fur stained the mechanism. I wasn't familiar with trapping but, by holding the steel trap with its coiled springs and leg crushing jaws, I knew I didn't care for it. Who would find enjoyment in placing such a contraption in the woods?

"It's not designed to kill. It just holds the animal until the trapper can dispatch it," Jason said.

"Dispatch?"

"Usually with a gun or club. The key is not to ruin the fur."

After sharing that tidbit of information, he wrapped the beagle in the towel and picked him up.

I tossed the trap into the carrier.

Dale said he was going to continue hiking north. After thanking him for his help, we headed back to the truck. I offered to take a turn carrying the beagle, but Jason said he could handle it. Like the drive, the walk was cloaked with an uncomfortable silence and that didn't change on the drive to town.

We took the dog to Dr. Katie Johnson, who did all the veterinarian work for the shelter but maintained a private practice as well. We left the beagle in the truck while we went in to talk to her.

Meg Hall was at the front desk. Besides Dr. Katie, Meg was the only other full-time person at the clinic. She was a jill-of-all-trades. Office work was her area of expertise, but she loved animals and could help the doctor where needed.

"We have a dog whose leg was caught in a trap. Does Dr. Katie have time to look at it?" I asked.

"I'm sure she'll make time," Meg said. "Take him to the exam room," she said, pointing down the hall to an open door. "I'll tell Dr. Katie what you have."

We went out to the truck. Jason said he'd carry the dog in if I opened the doors. The beagle's tail thumped on the seat as Jason petted him. "Here we go," he said as he slipped his arm around the dog trying not to bump the injured leg in order to minimize the pain. The blanket covered the leg, so I never got a good look at the injury, but I did notice a nasty smell when in the truck.

I closed the truck door and hurried ahead to open the clinic door. Inside, Jason gently laid the dog on the exam table. Meg looked at the leg and grimaced. "I'll be right back," she said.

A couple minutes later, Dr. Katie came in the room. "Meg said you have a beagle whose leg was caught in a trap?"

We told her the dog's story. She petted the beagle and removed the muzzle. "I don't think we need this," she said. Next, she lifted off the blanket. It only took her a second to arrive at a diagnosis.

"Gangrene. We'll have to take the leg," she said. "I hate leghold traps," she added.

Chapter 2

After we left the vet's office, Jason told me he'd deal with the trapper and asked if I'd look for the owner of the beagle.

"No problem," I said.

The first thing I did after he dropped me off at the shelter was to inform my boss, Cindi Owens, about what had happened. Cindi had started as a volunteer at the shelter and was hired as the director after the previous director had been caught stealing dogs. Cindi was also a friend. She, too, had been angry about the dog fighting incident but had been more understanding—understanding as a friend, that is—about the entire situation than Jason had been. As a boss, she had informed that me I would be on probation for the next six months.

"So, if anyone calls about a missing beagle, let me know," I said as I left her office.

I checked our logbook of lost and found pets. There hadn't been any calls for a beagle. Next, I checked Facebook where there were several groups, both locally and statewide, dedicated to lost and found pets. One was specific to our county. I didn't see any postings that matched my search criteria. Using a closeup photo of the beagle's face and another of his entire body, I wrote a found-post stating where the dog had been found and asked anyone who might recognize the dog to contact the animal shelter for more information.

Next, I searched online for information about trapping regulations in Michigan. What I learned made my stomach queasy. Anger burst from behind my composed demeanor; I pounded the desk with my fist and threw a stapler at the wall. What justified the way we treated wildlife? Like they were playthings put here for our amusement instead of sentient beings with lives to live.

That's when my awakening started to germinate.

With the work day coming to an end, I turned off the computer and started the routine of caring for the animals at the shelter. Luckily, volunteers walked the dogs throughout the day. All I had to do was spot clean, fill water bowls and hand out treats. With the cats, I scooped litter boxes and filled water and food bowls. The chores always took longer than expected, because the animals craved attention. I had to take a minute or two with each one. Back rubs, behind-the-ear scratches, belly tickles, kind words, whatever was requested.

Two years ago, I moved to Northern Michigan from the Chicago area to live with my grandmother, Anna, whom I called Grams. The move helped us both. Grams' husband, my grandfather, Tom Haley, had died, and I assumed she would be lonely and would need help on the farm.

For me, a fresh start was in order. The move helped me escape the death of my nine-year-old son, Thomas, from leukemia and the subsequent demise of my marriage.

Truth be told, Grams didn't need me as much as I needed her. As a kid, I had spent summers on the farm with my grandparents. My relationship was closer with them than with my parents.

Grams hadn't told me she hired someone to help on the farm after Gramps died. I thought she was trying to manage alone and needed help, that I would swoop in and be her savior, that I would land in a place where I was needed.

What funny games fate plays with us. At first I despised the man she hired but, wouldn't you know it, I fell in love with Mr. Cooper Malecki. Eventually he loved me too. He was much more than a hired hand though—he was the grandson of Gram's friend Lucia Malecki, and he was wanted for questioning regarding a fire at a horse slaughterhouse in California. We were both hiding from our past. But you can't run forever.

Cooper ended up pleading guilty and was sentenced to prison. Due to overcrowding, he was released early and placed on parole in California, which caused me a dilemma: stay in Michigan or move to California. Stay and help Grams, where I was now truly needed, or move west to be with my guy.

I couldn't leave Grams.

On the drive home, I noticed a store I had driven by hundreds of times without seeing the sign that read, "Hunting and Trapping Supplies." I slammed on the brakes but missed the driveway anyway. I turned around.

Not sure what to expect, I had to dare myself to go in. *Put on a smile and act like you belong.* So, I sauntered in like I owned the place. A balding man with a full beard and dressed in blue jeans and a plaid shirt stood behind a counter.

"What can I help you with, Missy?" he asked.

"I'm looking for a birthday present for my husband. The other day he was telling me about trapping with his father when he was a kid, and I thought maybe it would be a good hobby for him," I said. Making up stories, otherwise known as lying, was getting easier and easier. The proverbial slippery slope: once you start sliding, it's almost impossible to stop.

"Trapping is a good hobby—gets you outdoors and helps control the numbers of nuisance animals. Plus, you can sell the pelts and make a few bucks."

"What do you need to get started?"

"A few traps. A Knife. Does he have a gun?"

"What do you need a gun for?"

"To dispatch whatever is caught. The trap doesn't kill. It just holds the animals—that's why it's called a leghold trap." Some people use a club. You can use whatever you want, just so you don't damage the fur.

"He hunts, so he has a gun."

"Do you know what he needs?"

"To tell the truth, no. He might even have the traps he used as a kid. He's a packrat. Doesn't throw much away."

"Have you considered a gift card? Then he could get whatever he wants."

"That's an idea. I have a couple weeks to decide. Are there places to trap around here?"

"There's a trapping season. It's legal on private property with permission of the owner and in some state and national forests," he said.

Frank—that's what the guy's name tag said—handed me a booklet. "Read this. It has everything you need to know about trapping in Michigan. It's put out by the DNR.

"DNR?"

"Department of Natural Resources."

Next, Frank handed me a trap. "The jaws are designed to hold, not kill," Frank repeated. He took the trap from my hands and, without my asking for more information, gave me a detailed explanation of how it worked. Thankfully, another customer came in with a question and interrupted him. He handed the trap back to me. "I'll be right back," he said.

The steel felt cold and harsh in my hands. It didn't take much imagination to feel the pain and distress of a wild animal—coyote, bobcat, raccoon or possum—having a leg caught in such a vile invention.

Leaving the trap on the counter, I wandered around the store. There were books and DVDs, bait, skinning gloves, parts for traps, snares and starter kits for trapping raccoons and other animals. When I couldn't take it any longer, I found Frank, thanked him for his help and left. I was proud of myself for remaining civil while surrounded by disgusting merchandise for what I considered a morally corrupt, exploitive activity.

While sitting in the parking lot, I thumbed through the *Hunting and Trapping Digest* Frank had given me: season dates, bag limits, licenses, equipment regulations, youth hunting, small game, waterfowl, fur harvesting, baiting. The booklet was full of euphemisms: bag limit, harvest, sport. Why not use *kill*? Even Frank never used the word *kill*. Like Jason, he used *dispatch*.

The whole concept of animals being considered a natural resource bothered me. Trees were a natural resource. Minerals were a natural resource. Water was a natural resource. But animals? They were sentient beings who deserved better.

My awakening was taking root.

Chapter 3

Grams wasn't home. Her note said she had gone for groceries and would be back for dinner. The fur-babies were anxious to go outside. Cody, my German shepherd, and his side-kick, Shadow, bounced around in anticipation of my opening the door for them. Grams' dogs—Elvis and Sinatra—were a little more reserved in their begging for a potty break. Their tails wagged as they hovered near the door. Blue, my blind beagle, stood behind the other dogs, patiently waiting with his tail wagging. He knew the routine. Part of the yard was fenced-in so the dogs could run free, but they had to be supervised. We kept a close watch on the dogs ever since Cody and Blue had been stolen from the yard a couple years ago. Laws had been *sidestepped* to get them back––I used euphemisms too.

Sitting at the picnic table waiting for Grams and watching the dogs, I opened my laptop and surfed for more information about trapping. I discovered that trapping goes hand-in-hand with hunting. My searches kept pulling up different hunting preserves and ranches. Out of curiosity, I clicked on one just to see what they were about.

My awakening grew. The cliché, "ignorance is bliss," came to mind. What is seen, can't be unseen. What is learned, can't be unlearned.

Hunting preserves, I learned, consisted of fenced-in land where people pay to hunt. Whitetail deer, elk, buffalo, rams and wild pigs were on the menu, along with exotic breeds of deer unfamiliar to me. A six-point whitetail buck went for $750, and the price tag on an eight-point was $1,800. Prices went up to $3,500. Does were $350. People weren't hunting for food. They were trophy hunting.

"Our experienced staff will ensure you and your guests have the deer hunt of a lifetime ... time and time again! We have a trophy whitetail buck that is sure to get your heart pumping!"

Artic hogs started at $350. The bigger the animal, the higher the cost. Fees weren't listed for the exotic animals; it said to request pricing.

The hunts were guaranteed. Of course, they were. There's no escape for the animals when they were fenced-in. The preserves also provided lodging, taxidermy and meat processing. One review said, "It wasn't much of a hunt, but it was fun. We'll be back."

Who finds killing fenced-in animals fun? Where's the hunt? It's just cold-blooded slaughter. Just reading about it and seeing the photos of men and, to my surprise, women and kids displaying huge smiles posed next to dead animals made my stomach queasy.

To my dismay, one of the whitetail preserves was in my county. Even worse, there were several throughout the state. Even birds had targets on their backs. Some preserves were devoted to pheasants, quail and, yes, mallard ducks. Exotic game birds could be taken year-round. *Taken*––another euphemism for kill.

Luckily, the sound of Grams' car pulling in the driveway interrupted my education. I met her at the car and carried in the bags of groceries.

Our normal routine was barn duty, then dinner. Besides the dogs, we had three horses, a pregnant cow and several barn cats.

"I bought the fixings for veggie lasagna, so I'll cook if you do chores," Grams said.

She knew I preferred being in the barn to the kitchen. "It's a deal," I said. "How much time do I have?"

"More than an hour."

With an hour, I could go for a quick ride plus do the feedings. According to the calendar, summer was over, but warm temperatures had me in denial. But there was no denying winter was approaching with the sun setting earlier and earlier. Maples, with their occasional splash of red leaves, hinted that a change of season was upon us.

Down at the barn I whistled, and Dappy, Chester and

MaryLu came cantering across the pasture. They knew a whistle meant food. Bessie, the dairy cow who had escaped an overturned truck on the way to slaughter, was part of the herd too. With her bulging belly, she wasn't one to run, but she did amble her way to the barn.

Carrots were the treat of the day. As they munched, I went in the barn and got a bridle. I slipped it over Dappy's head. He was my horse. Chester belonged to my late grandpa and MaryLou was Grams' horse.

For this ride, I left the dogs under Grams' supervision. A trail behind the barn provided a quick jaunt to the river. No saddle this time; I preferred bareback. It was hard to hold Dappy to a trot; he was anxious to stretch his legs. When we had an open stretch with no low-hanging branches, I urged him to canter. As we approached the bend that led to the river, I slowed him to a walk. When we neared the water, we spooked three deer: two does and a buck. Dappy stopped as they ran down the path in front of us. The beauty of the moment was spoiled by the memory of the websites. What mentality found it acceptable, even enjoyable, to kill such beautiful creatures? It left me mystified.

The sweet, spicy aroma of tomatoes, garlic and oregano greeted me when I got back to the house. The table was set, wine poured and salad served.

"It's out of the oven and has to set for a few minutes before it can be cut," Grams announced.

While it wasn't appetizing table talk, Grams and I discussed trapping over dinner. Gramps hadn't been a trapper, so she didn't know much about it. I told her about the dog and how his leg had to be amputated.

"It sounds like a cruel sport," she said.

Another euphemism. Baseball was a sport. Football was a sport. Sport was supposed to be fun, entertaining, a competition of skill. While hunting may be all those things for the hunter, the animal being hunted most likely didn't find it fun or entertaining.

"I find it pretty disgusting," I said.

"I guess it's one of the downsides of living in the country—

you're more aware of nature, and it's not always pretty," Grams said.

"You're right about that," I agreed, pouring myself another glass of wine.

After we cleaned up the kitchen, I called Cooper. At least his probation gave us the chance to talk every night. Discussing our day was the perfect nightcap. He was saddened but realistic about my beagle story.

"At least he's alive. I knew a guy who owned a three-legged dog. The dog didn't have a problem getting around and didn't seem to have any issues. Animals don't feel sorry for themselves," he said trying to comfort me.

"True, but it makes me angry that traps are being set for wild animals. It's cruel and unfair," I said.

"The real problem is that humans are destroying and moving into wild places. Then they complain about critters eating their flowers or getting in their garbage. Nobody wants to face the real problem—too many people," Cooper said.

Cooper always had a different perspective on things, which I didn't always agree with. Too many people? Was that the real problem?

Chapter 4

The next day on the way into work, I stopped at the vet's office to check on the beagle. I was early enough that Dr. Katie didn't have clients yet. She led me to the back to see the patient.

"He didn't have a microchip," she said, holding the door open for me. "It would have been nice to find one so we could have gotten permission from the owner for treatment."

"You removed his leg?"

"We had to. There was too much damage and infection. Dogs get along fine on three legs. Any luck finding the owner?"

"Not yet, but I've been posting online. If no one comes forward, we'll find him a new home."

Dr. Katie opened the kennel and rubbed the dog's head. "He's a friendly guy," she said.

"Do you think he's a house dog or somebody's hunting dog?" I asked.

"Hard to tell. Maybe both."

"How long does he have to be here?"

"A couple days, but if you're just going to take him to the shelter, he can stay here a few extra days. I think he'll do better here."

I squatted down, and the dog came over to me for attention. I rubbed between his ears. "Sounds good," I agreed. "I'll keep looking for his owner."

The door to backroom opened and Meg stepped in. "Dr. Katie, your first client is here," she said.

Dr. Katie asked Meg to put the beagle back in his kennel and then excused herself.

Meg came over to us and knelt down. "He's such a good dog,"

she commented. "So happy."

Being alone with Meg afforded the privacy to ask how she was doing. A few weeks earlier, she had confided in me that she was going through a divorce.

"Divorce is a tough time," I said. "If there's anything I can do to help, just call. Or if you need someone to talk to, I'm always available. Maybe we could go to dinner sometime."

She appreciated the offer. She said her sister and Dr. Katie were supportive, and she felt good about things. "They gave me the courage to leave him. After five years, I realized he wasn't going to change, and I couldn't change him," she said. The words sounded good, but her voice was slow and hesitant, like she was repeating something from memory.

"It'll get better," I said. "It takes time but, believe me, it'll get better." I gave her a hug.

"Thanks," she whispered. "I appreciate your kindness."

Jason was at the shelter when I arrived. He told me that, from the name on the trap, he was able to locate the owner.

"Did you ticket him?" I asked.

"For what? It wasn't his fault the dog got caught."

"I thought you said the trap should have been staked down."

"It was, but the dog apparently pulled it loose. I told him he needed to do a better job of securing his traps."

"That's it?"

"Yup. Trapping is legal this time of year."

"I picked up the DNR's guide for hunting and trapping." As soon as I said it, I regretted it.

"Why?" Jason asked in a raised voice. His hands were on his hips.

"Because I don't know much about it and thought I should."

"You don't need to know about it. *I* do. All you need to do is worry about cats and dogs."

"You're right," I agreed. Changing the subject, I gave him a progress report on locating the beagle's owner. "I stopped and checked on the dog this morning, and he's doing okay. They amputated the leg, but the prognosis is good."

The encounter didn't do anything to improve our relationship.

That night after dinner with Grams, I again looked at websites for hunting preserves. I discovered several organizations that condemned the practice, calling them "captive hunts" and "canned hunts."

I was astonished to learn that in South Africa guaranteed hunts for lions were popular. A hunt for a full-grown, captive-bred male lion could cost $30,000 or more. A lion with a dark, thick mane was listed for $55,000. Lionesses could be had for $6,000 or less. It was even possible to shoot lion cubs.

"Unbelievable!" I shouted at the screen. Cody, Shadow and Blue, who were sleeping by my feet, jumped at my loud voice. They stared at me in anticipation of what I'd do next.

"How did the world get so crazy?" I asked them. Cody got to his feet, his tail wagging as if in agreement.

I read on.

Animals killed in captive hunts came from private breeders, animal dealers, circuses and even zoos. Zoos? Everyone loves baby animals. People flock to zoos to see the baby snow leopards, lions and tigers. I never thought of it before, but what happens to all those babies when they grow up? Is it possible they were sold to hunting preserves?

The hunted animals were frequently hand-raised and bottle-fed, meaning they lost their fear of people. Some farmers who bred and raised lions for hunts called themselves conservationists. They were even open to tourists who loved seeing the cubs. Photo opportunities.

According to the Humane Society of the United States, captive hunting is a lucrative and expanding industry. They estimated that more than 1,000 captive-mammal hunting operations were operating in at least two dozen states. Several factors fed into that expansion: the overbreeding of captive exotic animals, the desire by wealthy hunters for a quick and easy kill for bragging rights, and the incentive to bag exotic mammals provided by Safari Club International's trophy-hunting-achievement award.

My awakening continued, but now my anger was growing. What to do about it? I felt compelled to learn more. A calling from God?

I needed to see for myself. I emailed one of the nearby hunting preserves and asked if I could have a tour, that I was interested in buying a hunt for my husband for his birthday. Fake husbands do come in handy. A reply came within minutes. Anytime tomorrow morning would be okay.

Chapter 5

After the morning routine of caring for the animals at the shelter, I checked emails and social media. One of the messages was from a guy named Stanley. He was missing a beagle. He included his phone number. I called him immediately.

Stanley described the coloring of his dog and said that he was wearing a leather collar without tags. The beagle's name was Buster. He had been chasing a rabbit and disappeared into the woods and was gone.

My thoughts quickly turned judgmental. *Rabbit hunting? Who finds pleasure in killing docile bunnies? Where does the insanity end?*

I told him that Buster had been caught in a leghold trap, and we had taken him to a vet. "Unfortunately, his leg was beyond repair and had to be amputated."

"You what? You cut off his leg? How's he gonna run with three legs?" Stanley yelled.

"Dr. Johnson said dogs get along fine with three legs." Then I added gravy to the unsettling news. "You'll be responsible for the vet bill."

"I ain't paying no vet bill! You crippled my dog!" he bellowed.

I matched his anger with fury of my own. "No, we didn't ruin your dog. We saved his life. He could have died if we hadn't rescued him. He would have died from gangrene if his leg hadn't been amputated. If you don't pay the bill, he'll become the property of the county. We'll find him a new home."

The phone went dead. I smiled. We'd find Buster a home worthy of him, a home with a fenced yard so he wouldn't get lost again. But I had a problem--I really needed Stanley's signature on a release form. I didn't want him changing his mind. So I called him back. He didn't answer.

After telling Cindi about the conversation, I asked if I could take a couple hours off to run an errand. She didn't mind. Forty-five minutes later, I pulled into the driveway of the Great Northern Whitetail and Wild Boar Ranch. A man came out of the house as I parked. He introduced himself as Eddie Hunter.

"Yes, Hunter is my last name. I was destined for this," he said with a chuckle as he spread out his arms as if to encompass the ranch.

I nodded my head and laughed. "Seems that way. I'm Susan Hartwick. I messaged you last night." Not sure where I came up with the name Susan, but Hartwick was my best friend, Sara's, last name.

"You're interested in a hunt for your husband?"

"I am."

What's his name?

"Rob," I said. The name rolled out of my mouth with ease. Rob was my ex-husband.

Eddie took me to his office, which was in a pole barn. He handed me two brochures. "One is for our whitetail hunts, the other for wild boar. We also offer taxidermy. That was my business before I started the ranch," he explained.

He led the way into his display room. Watching from the walls were six deer heads, each with majestic antlers. I felt their embarrassment at having been decapitated and admired only for their antlers. I felt the sadness of their captivity, of being forever inside never to feel the intensity of the sun, a gentle rain or the briskness of winter.

A full deer posed next to his desk. The buck's eyes stared at me as if pleading. For what? To be alive again? To be returned to the wild?

"They're beauties, aren't they?" Eddie asked. "They were all born, raised and harvested here."

Harvest, the favorite euphemism of hunters.

"Really?" was all I could think to say.

"In this room we have the wild boars," he said as he opened a door and held it for me to go through.

An entire wild boar, which looked like a pig to me, stood in a corner. On the walls were heads with protruding tusks.

"The wild boars come in a variety of colors," Eddie explained. "Black, dark gray, brown, red and spotted. Something for every décor," he said with a laugh.

"Color matters?" I asked.

"To some guys it does."

He handed me another brochure. This one on the taxidermy service. "Most just go with the head. An entire boar gets pricey, but it's an option. We can also process the meat. If you don't want it, we can donate it to a food bank."

I didn't know what to say so I lowered my head to study the brochure.

"Any questions?"

"Not really. The brochures seem to cover everything."

"Would you like a tour of the ranch?"

"Sure. Is it safe?"

"We'll be inside the truck. Totally safe."

Eddie explained the ranch had fenced-in areas for the younger animals that weren't ready to be harvested. There were two 100-acre hunt areas where the animals were kept that were suitable for harvest: one for whitetail and one for wild boar. "We keep them separate for the hunters. We'll go see the boars first."

I couldn't believe it when Eddie said the wild boars knew the difference between the pickup, which they associated with being fed, and the jeep that the hunters used.

"They're smart. When they see the jeep, they run. It makes it a little more work for the hunters, which is what they expect. They want it easy, but not *too* easy." He chuckled at his attempt at humor. I managed a slight laugh.

Most of the boars were laying down in the shade of a maple tree. They weren't too interested in us. Eddie was right about the variety of colors. They were beautiful.

"They're not too wild. They don't live up to their name," I said.

"I already fed them this morning so they're full," Eddie said. "On the days we hunt, they don't get fed. Makes them a little more restless, more aggressive. They don't like missing a meal. It makes them a little angry. It helps put on a good show for the hunters."

The deer weren't quite as tame. They kept their distance and moved away as we got closer. They probably felt safe, but a modern-day rifle with a scope could easily dispatch a bullet to their heart.

"They're beautiful," I said.

"Do you think your husband would enjoy hunting here?" Eddie asked.

"I bet he would. The last few times he's gone out on public land he hasn't gotten anything. He sees a few does but no bucks. He's always disappointed."

"We'd love to have him join us on a hunt. All our hunts are guided and guaranteed. He won't be disappointed here."

I told Eddie I was tempted to buy a gift hunt, but the way my husband was with money, I thought I'd better wrap a brochure and let him decide which hunt he wanted.

"I want Robbie to be happy, not mad. He can be hard to please."

"Let me know what he decides," Eddie said.

My thoughts were jumbled on the drive back to the shelter, but I had three revelations.

First, I couldn't believe Eddie was so nonchalant about what he was doing. That he believed hunting fenced-in animals who had no escape was acceptable.

Second, that there were enough people who liked captive hunting to keep him in business.

Third, that I was able to keep my composure when I felt like screaming, "How can you be so heartless?" In my mind, it was wrong, sinful.

Chapter 6

I had two unexpected phone calls that afternoon. The first was from my mother inviting me to visit. My parents lived in a suburb of Chicago, which was where I had grown up. I had spent summers in Northern Michigan with my grandparents, and it didn't take long for me to conclude that I wasn't a city girl. Something neither parent could understand.

Mom admitted she had an ulterior motive for the invitation. "We're having all the walls repainted. I decided to minimize, so I'm sorting through everything. You still have several boxes of stuff in the storage room."

She wanted me to come and get my belongings. To be honest, I couldn't even remember what the boxes contained. Some of the stuff was from my childhood, and the rest had been stored there since I moved to Michigan. Of course, she wanted everything out immediately. My mother had no patience, and she was stubborn—an uncomplimentary combination. Long ago I learned that arguing with her was like trying to stop a runaway train. Her mind couldn't be changed, and the train was going to run you over, most likely not even noticing you.

"Can you come this weekend?" she asked.

I didn't have plans for the weekend so I told her yes.

Coincidently, the second call was also from Chicago: Rocky Pahn, the founder and director of Friends not Fighters. The group rehabilitated fighting dogs and had taken some of the animals from the dog fighting ring that I helped bust. Mike, one of the volunteers from Friends, had been killed in the fiasco.

Mike had been raised in a culture that normalized dog fighting, but he learned to despise the tradition. Mike's dad invited him to Michigan to watch a young pit bull named Diesel perform in his first match.

Disguised as a man, I had gone to that fight with Mike. Long story short: three people died that night: Mike, his dad Vic and Sheriff Marc VanBergen. Mike died because he couldn't stomach watching Diesel in a death battle. He loved that dog.

One of the dogs that Friends not Fighters took was Diesel. Rocky promised me the option of adopting Diesel if the dog's training could be reversed. The guilt and grief that consumed me after Mike's death left me with a sense of obligation to give the dog a home.

"Hey, Rocky, good to hear from you. What's up?" I asked.

"Just wanted to let you know how Diesel is doing."

"Is he okay?"

"He's doing better than okay. He took to the retraining, probably because of his age, and he's ready to go to a new home. Are you still interested in adopting him?"

I paused for a moment. Did I really want another dog? Did I want a pit bull? I admit the negative stories the media bombarded everyone with regarding pit bulls left me on edge. "Can he be trusted with other dogs and with cats?" I asked.

"Yes, but I would keep an eye on him. Introduce him slowly," Rocky said. "We wouldn't let him leave if we didn't think he was ready."

I told Rocky I just happened to be going to Chicago that weekend and could stop by. "Can I meet him before I decide?" I asked.

"Sure. When are you thinking?"

"Would Sunday work? I'll stop by on my way back to Michigan." We arranged for me to call him when I was about an hour out.

After hanging up, I sat back in my chair to think about what I had just agreed to. Two phone calls and my weekend was booked. Sorting through boxes of whatever it was I left behind would dredge up memories, which I didn't relish. Dealing with Diesel would do the same.

On my day's to-do list was "check on Buster the beagle." Instead of calling, I drove to the clinic.

"He's becoming a favorite," Meg said as she took me to the backroom. She opened the kennel and snapped a leash on his collar.

"Buster," I called to him. His tail wagged at hearing his name.

"Buster, it *is* you," I said. He rushed to me, walking on three legs with no hesitation. I rubbed his head and back as I told Meg the owner had been found but surrendered ownership to the county.

"He didn't think a three-legged dog would be able to chase rabbits. Probably an excuse for not paying the bill," I said.

"Animals adapt better to their disabilities than the owners do," she said. She assured me it was okay if he stayed for the weekend. "If he's going to be up for adoption, I'd be interested in him," she said. "He's such a sweetheart."

"Really? That would be perfect. Think about it, and we'll talk Monday."

Meg's offer to adopt the dog gave me satisfaction in my work. Helping animals in their time of need warmed my heart. I was tempted to adopt him too, but how many dogs could I bring home?

I had brought surrender paperwork with me, so I drove on out to Stanley Jones' home. I also brought a copy of the veterinarian bill.

An old black pickup was in his driveway when I pulled in. I turned off my car and got out, papers in hand, and headed to the house. I nearly jumped out of my skin when the truck's horn blared. I turned and noticed someone sitting in the driver's seat. Whoever it was didn't get out as I walked toward the truck. I noted the driver's side of the truck was scraped and dented, as if it had sideswiped another vehicle. The driver was a scruffy old man wearing a woodsy, camouflaged baseball cap. I introduced myself and asked if Stanley Jones was around. He stared, making me feel uneasy.

"What'd ya want?" he asked.

"Are you Mr. Jones?" He grunted something resembling a yes. "I need your signature releasing the beagle to us."

I handed the paper to him. To my surprise, he took it. After looking over the form, he folded it in half. Then he slowly tore it. He stacked the two pieces of paper together and tore again. He continued to rip the paper until only small shreds remained. Then he stuck his hand outside his window and let go of the pieces of paper, which floated to the ground like confetti.

"I ain't signing no papers," he growled.

"Okay then. Your verbal word will be used to relinquish your rights."

"I ain't relinquishing my rights."

"You did yesterday. On the phone."

"Get off my property," he barked. "Now!"

"Here's what you owe before you can pick up Buster," I said, handing him the bill. This time he didn't accept the paperwork. I let it fall into the truck. Without another word, I left, ever so thankful to get away from him.

That night over dinner, I invited Grams to go to Chicago with me. After all, my mother was her daughter.

She laughed. "No thanks. Don't even try to talk me into it." She had the same stubborn streak as my mother. Must be hereditary. Had it been passed on to me? If it had, I didn't notice it.

Grams had made us spaghetti with marinara sauce and no meatballs, salad and garlic bread. An Italian meal wouldn't be complete without red wine.

Grams ate a plant based diet. Cooper did too, but he called it vegan. They both conspired to make me quit eating meat, eggs and dairy. When they did the cooking, I gladly ate whatever they set down in front of me. Slowly, I was beginning to understand their reasoning. Maybe that family gene for stubbornness, which I refused to believe I inherited, was losing its grip. For a long time, I refused to change my diet, but I was finally getting it. Animals weren't ours to eat. Didn't matter that the Bible gave us dominion over them. Dominion didn't translate to killing. After all, wasn't one of the ten commandments, "Thou shall not kill"?

After Grams refused my invitation, I told her the second reason for my trip to the big city. "Is it okay to bring a pit bull to the farm?" I asked. "Do we dare trust a dog who was trained to fight?"

Grams loved dogs. She used to board dogs and understood the traits of the different breeds. "Pit bulls get a bad rap. I don't have a problem with the breed. If you decide to bring him here, we'll treat him like any newcomer. We'll keep him separated until we feel comfortable."

The decision was mine according to Grams. The farm would someday be mine. The animals would be my responsibility. If I wanted to fill the barn and house with pets, nothing would please her more. After our visit to SASHA Farm in Southern Michigan, we often talked about turning the farm into a sanctuary for animals.

I called Cooper after dinner. I missed that man. Our evening telephone talks were precious, but a weak substitute for being together.

Chapter 7

I didn't have to pack much for the trip to Chicago, which was good, because the car would be full on the trip home. I did take a large dog kennel. I kissed Grams goodbye and hit the road at nine o'clock. I'd be at my parents' by midafternoon.

After only an hour of driving, boredom set in. On a whim, I decided to call my friend Sara Hartwick, the friend whose last name I borrowed at Great Northern Whitetail Ranch. She lived with her husband, Ryan, in Grand Haven, a town on the east coast of Lake Michigan. "Friend" wasn't the right word to describe Sara. She was a *best* friend, a confidant. We had a bond as strong as sisters, maybe even identical twins.

I dialed her number.

"I can't believe it. I was just thinking about you," she said when she recognized my hello.

"Maybe that's why I had a sudden urge to call," I said with a laugh.

She laughed too. "How are things? When can we get together?" she asked.

"How about in thirty minutes? I'm on my way to Chicago and could meet for a quick coffee. Do you have time?"

"I can make time. Do you want to meet at Morning Star Café? It shouldn't be too busy now that the snowbirds and tourists are gone."

"Perfect. I'm just north of Muskegon. I should be there around ten thirty."

Sara had helped me when Blue and Cody had been stolen. If it hadn't been for her, Cooper would probably be in prison in Michigan. She also saved my butt when I went undercover to the

33

dog fight. As we had prearranged, she had called for help when I didn't report in. Her logical thinking always helped me put things into perspective. Maybe she could sprinkle some magical words on my obsession with the war on wildlife and suppress my awakening. Life would be easier if I could stop the fixation.

My old Subaru sported a CD player. The musical selection for this trip was oldies, beginning with the greatest hits of Gordon Lightfoot. Easy-listening, mellow folk music, somewhat melancholic. Perfect for my mood. "Sundown" and "Cotton Jenny" caught my ear, but my all-time favorite song was "The Wreck of the Edmund Fitzgerald." My favorite line is, "Does anyone know where the love of God goes when the waves turn the minutes to hours?" There were countless times when I wondered why God seemed to be missing in action. The old standby, "He works in mysterious ways," didn't cut it. Why was there so much suffering, both with humans and animals? Why did little boys die? Why did my Thomas have to die? Such questions bubbled to the surface with melancholic music.

When I arrived at the café, Sara already had a table and a pot of coffee. She greeted me with a bear hug and asked my reason for coming to Chicago.

"To help mother declutter. She's starting with my stuff. Plus, I might be bringing Mike's dog, Diesel, home with me," I told her.

Sara had briefly met Mike, and she thought he would be pleased with my adopting Diesel. "Mike gave his life to save Diesel. Giving him a second chance is the perfect tribute," she said.

I nodded in agreement as I stared into my coffee. "I replay that night over and over in my head wondering what I could have done differently."

"That's a waste of time. You have to quit thinking about it. It's done. It can't be changed. Learn from it and go forward."

She was right. I changed the subject to Buster and explained my awakening to trapping and captive hunting. "Not that I like any hunting, but at least in the wild the animals have a chance of escape," I said. I told her about the tour of the Whitetail Ranch.

"Why did you go?" she asked.

"It was so unbelievable that I had to see it with my own eyes."

"And now that you've seen it?"

"I don't know. Am I the only one bothered by it? Aren't you?"

Sara said she didn't care for trapping or hunting, but as long as it was legal, she wasn't concerned. "There are a lot of things in this world I don't like—war, people starving to death, kids dying of preventable diseases—but there's not much I can do about it," she concluded. "Hunting and trapping is tradition. You're not going to change that."

"You might be right, but shouldn't we try? You know what they say, 'be the change you want to see in the world. Change begins with you. Don't underestimate what one woman can do.'"

Sara laughed. "Not sure you got those right, but I get your sentiment. So, what are you proposing?"

I shook my head. "I don't know. I don't. It's overwhelming. You know what else I saw? The DNR is holding a trapping workshop for kids. I couldn't believe it. Kids! They're teaching them how to trap weasels. Teaching them that animals are something to be harvested, like corn or apples."

"You're a teacher. Go back to teaching. Teach kids how to treat animals right. One person can make a difference," she said.

I had been a teacher. When Thomas was diagnosed with leukemia, I took a leave of absence and never went back. I couldn't handle being around kids the same age as Thomas. I couldn't handle watching them grow up when Thomas never would.

Time sped by with Sara, and it wasn't long before I needed to get back on the road. I realized my life had dominated the conversation, so I changed the subject. "What's happening with you?"

Sara had been waiting for me to ask. She had huge news. She was pregnant.

"Pregnant," I echoed. "I'm so happy for you."

"We didn't plan it, but now that it's happened, we're excited."

"You should be. You guys will be awesome parents. I'm so jealous."

And I was. I recalled my pregnancy and how fabulous being a mother had been. After Thomas passed, I couldn't fathom having another child. But the instant Sara shared her news, I knew I wanted more children. Living without kids produced its own pain.

Chapter 8

"Make three piles. Stuff to keep. Stuff to toss. Stuff to donate. Goodwill is coming Monday. They'll take anything we don't want," Mom said as she led me to the spare bedroom she used for storage. There were boxes and plastic tubs stacked from floor to ceiling, filling close to half the room.

"This can't be all mine," I said.

"No, dear, some of it's mine. I thought it would be fun to work together. I'll be right back." She disappeared, leaving me alone to face the intimidating task.

My mother drove me nuts. I still marveled at the fact that she was Grams' daughter. How that happened baffled me. Certain genetic traits must have skipped a generation. Mom's decision to become a minimalist was just another keeping-up-with-the-Joneses performance. Truth be told, I just didn't want to be hassled with going through the boxes of junk I had deposited at her house years ago. Stuff I should have tossed or donated, but couldn't. There were too many memories.

"Have a glass of wine. It'll help," Mom said on her return. She carried a tray with an opened bottle of wine in a chiller and two crystal wine glasses. I even disliked the way she served wine: a tray, a stainless-steel wine chiller and crystal. Too snobbish for me. Grams would have felt the same.

We spent the afternoon drinking, sorting and reminiscing. A few boxes contained pre-marriage clothes, books and childhood mementos. The clothes were outdated and easy to part with. I kept a few books. The stuff from my childhood was harder to part with, but who needed old school papers, high school art projects and trophies from track? Yes, I used to be a runner.

The boxes that were harder to face were the ones I stored after the divorce when I moved to Michigan. Kitchen gadgets that neither Rob nor I wanted, more books, photo albums and boxes of dresses. Yes, I used to wear dresses.

More books went in the keep pile, as did the photo albums that I wasn't ready to look at yet. To my surprise, one of the boxes contained a fur coat. I couldn't believe it, a fur coat I had forgotten about. Rob's grandmother insisted I take it the last time we visited her. Looking back, she must have had a premonition about her death and was cleaning house. She had had a heart attack and died a month later.

The coat had been a birthday gift to her from her husband. She whispered to me that she never wanted a fur coat but wore it to make her husband happy; it made him feel successful that he could afford to buy her a fur.

I tried it on. Something I would have never done if I hadn't been drinking.

"I didn't know you had a fur. When did you get that?" Mom asked as she ran her hand over the plush garment.

"Rob's grandmother gave it to me. It's the only thing I have of hers," I said.

Memories of Rob's Polish grandmother, Busia, flooded my mind: her serving us tea and store-bought chocolate chip cookies and her dog who had followed her home from the market one day. The owners had never been found, so she gladly kept the sheltie. Without being taught, the dog became her ears as her hearing faded. If the doorbell rang, he would jump up and bark at the door, her cue to answer it. When the tea kettle on the stove whistled, he barked at her. I would have loved to have her dog when she died, but a grandson claimed him.

The full-length coat was a reddish brown and so soft. I petted it like I would a dog. I didn't want it, but I couldn't part with Busia's memory. The coat went in the keep pile.

In Mom's boxes, we found clothing, costume jewelry and the accumulated stuff from years of travel, shopping and Christmases.

"Hey, I gave that to you," I said, picking up a coffee-table book of scenes from Chicago.

"And I loved it, and I looked at it."

I put it in the donate pile.

"See if you want any of my jewelry," Mom said, handing me a box.

Inside were dozens of small plastic baggies, each holding a single item. A red necklace caught my eye. I tried it on but resisted the urge to keep it. I tried on a couple rings and bracelets too, but her style wasn't mine. Besides, I seldom wore jewelry.

"I think it's all destined for donation," I said, putting the necklace back in its plastic bag.

"Do it," she said, not wanting to take responsibility for giving away what was once treasured by her.

I put the box in the donation pile.

She was right about one thing: the wine helped. We laughed, shared stories and advised each other on what to keep and what to part with. It had been a long time since I had enjoyed my mother's company like I did that afternoon.

By the time we finished, Dad was home from golfing. Nobody felt like cooking, so Dad offered to take us out. Mom suggested Mexican. There was a new restaurant nearby that offered vegetarian dishes. I ordered a vegan burrito, which paired nicely with sangria.

All the alcohol made for an early bedtime. Once in my room, I called Cooper. The thing most heavily on my mind was Sara and her news. My insight of wanting more children clung to the tip of my tongue. I shared Sara's news. The alcohol gave me courage, so I asked the question: "Do you ever see us having kids?" Then I held my breath, wishing I could see his face, his eyes.

"Wow," he said. "You got me ... do you want kids? I thought you didn't."

"I didn't. After Thomas died, I didn't. But hearing Sara's news ... something changed. I found myself feeling jealous. Just like that, I wanted a baby."

"I always thought I'd have kids someday, but haven't thought about it lately," he said. "So, I guess my answer is yes, someday."

His answer terrified me.

The next morning, I loaded the car with the keep pile, which easily fit beside the dog kennel. After a quick breakfast, I kissed my parents goodbye, set my GPS to Rocky's address and hit the road.

Chapter 9

As I drove, my cell phone dinged with a text message, but I didn't dare take my eyes off the multiple lanes of I-90 and the cars that dodged in and out of lanes. I felt like a driver in a video game. Then the phone rang, no way could I answer it. Whoever wanted to talk to me would have to wait a few minutes.

A couple miles from Rocky's place, I noticed a cloud of smoke in the distance. There was no reason to connect it to the text and phone call, but as I got closer, I started to wonder. A block from my destination, the police had the road blocked off. Billowy black smoke spewed from the roof of Rocky's kennel. I parked, grabbed my phone and checked the messages.

"Fire at our kennel," the text read. Rocky had left a voice message too. His voice quivered as he spoke. "Our building is on fire. I don't know if all the dogs got out. No need to come today. Talk to you later."

I felt sick to my stomach. How horrible. I texted him back saying I was already here and parked by the road block.

I got out of the car and talked to one of the officers blocking the road. He wouldn't tell me anything and wouldn't let me through. My phone dinged. The text said Rocky was on his way to meet me.

He came bumbling along the sidewalk with three dogs on leads. The officer let me through the roadblock to go meet him.

"I'm so sorry," I said as I gave him a hug. He didn't want to let go. After a few seconds, he regained his composure and pulled away, his face stained with tears.

"Jim, whose turn it was to spend the night with the dogs, smelled smoke and called 9-1-1. He called me, and I got here as fast as I could. He got burned pretty bad trying to get the dogs out so they took him to the hospital. We still don't know if he got everybody out. He put three in his car. I found two tied to trees. We found a couple wondering loose."

"How many are missing?"

"Two, I think. Can you hold these guys so I can keep looking?" he asked, handing me the tangle of leashes.

As we talked, another car pulled up to the police barricade. Rocky waved to the officer, indicating he knew the driver so he would let him though.

"It's Vincent, one of rehabbers," Rocky said. He greeted his friend with a bear hug and then recapped what was happening as we walked toward the smoldering structure. A small group of neighbors gathered to watch.

"I'll wait back here," I told Rocky as I struggled to hold the leashes of the distracted and confused dogs.

"We need to find the last two," Rocky said. "I'll be back in a few minutes."

Firefighters were spraying water on the building, which was partially collapsed. If any dogs remained inside, I doubted if they were alive. As I watched the horrific scene, I felt a sharp tug on the leashes. I switched my attention to the dogs in my safekeeping. All three of them strained against their collars toward a brick house. Then I noticed what they were fixated on: two black pit-bull-type dogs stood about ten feet away from us. They didn't growl or show signs of aggression, but their statue-like stance and no-emotion stare chilled my sense of safety. Were they Rocky's dogs or neighborhood strays?

"Do you know these guys," I asked my leashed companions, trying hard not to reveal my fear. I tugged on their leashes to bring them closer to me, but they ignored me. Their combined strength was no match for mine.

Time stood still. On the outside, calmness prevailed, but inside, panic gripped me. I wasn't sure what to do. Where was Rocky? I slowly pulled my phone from my pocket and sent him a one-word text: "Help."

"Let's go," I said as I jerked the leashes. The dogs didn't want to leave, and I wasn't a physical match for three bully-breed dogs.

So we stayed.

It probably wasn't forever, but that's how long it seemed to take Rocky to return.

"Bubbles. Babe. Come," he said. Then he turned to me. "Those are the two we've been looking for." As soon as the dogs heard their names, they obeyed Rocky's command and trotted toward him. He squatted down and hugged both dogs at the same time. He cried, but this time happy tears. He wiped his face on his sleeve as he stood up. "They're all okay," he said in disbelief. "Jim got them all out."

"Bubbles and Babe?" I teased.

He chuckled. "We give them gentle names, not fighting names."

"Did you rename Diesel?"

"We've been calling him Buddy, but you can call him anything you want. He's in Jim's car."

Vincent came with leashes and greeted the two dogs with affection. Then he hugged Rocky. "We'll survive this," I heard him whisper. "I'm sure our volunteers will foster until we regroup," Vincent said. "I can take Bubbles and Babe." He reached down and rubbed their heads again.

"I'll be taking Diesel ... I mean Buddy," I said.

Vincent turned to me. "Now I know who you are," he said. "Mike was a friend. When I heard what he had done, I wasn't surprised. When someone sees the light, so to speak, they usually go overboard in the opposite direction. That was Mike. He had no tolerance for people who abused dogs, and no doubt he saw dog fighting as abuse. It tore him up that his father was involved."

"I'm so sorry for what happened," I said. "I only met him the once, but I knew his heart. He didn't deserve to die."

Rocky put his arm around me. "We're all sorry for what happened. We still miss him, but life goes on. Now he's our inspiration," he said. "Let's get Buddy for you. You have a long drive, and we have to figure out what we're doing next."

Buddy was a bundle of energy when Rocky let him out of Jim's car. Being enclosed in a vehicle was probably a new experience for him, not to mention watching and hearing the commotion of the firefighters and noise of the fire engines.

"Buddy, sit," Rocky said. Buddy sat, but his body quivered with excitement. "I think he needs a walk before he goes on a long car ride."

Vincent offered to watch the other dogs while Rocky and I took Buddy for a walk. "I'll make some calls and round up people to take the dogs," he said.

On our walk, we commiserated over Mike's death and the fire.

"I'll bet anything it was arson," Rocky said. He took the fire as a sign that they were having an impact. "If they didn't feel threatened, they'd leave us alone."

"Who's 'they'?" I asked.

"I don't know. Whoever has something to lose if we convince people dog fighting is wrong."

"Maybe you should move to a safer neighborhood," I said.

"No, we need to be visible here. This is where kids are being taught that dog fighting is acceptable. We have to be a voice for the dogs. We'll be more cautious from now on. We need surveillance cameras. Maybe we need to have two people stay with the dogs instead of one."

The fire had strengthened his resolve to continue the fight.

Using Buddy as an example, I could attest to the fact that Rocky knew what he was doing. Buddy walked well on a leash and obeyed commands. He lived to please.

Rocky and Vincent walked me to my car. They teared up as they said goodbye to Buddy.

"We get attached," Vincent said, giving the squirming Buddy one last hug.

"I'm not surprised. If you ever get to Michigan, feel free to visit him," I said. "You're both welcome anytime."

"Don't be surprised if we show up some time," Rocky said.

Without hesitation, Buddy jumped into my car and then ducked down into the kennel. I hugged Vincent and Rocky goodbye.

What a weekend. I couldn't wait to get back to my life in Michigan.

Chapter 10

Buddy didn't make a sound all the way home. I debated taking him for a walk at a rest area but worried about handling him in a public place. The stigma of his breed lingered.

When I got home, Grams and the dogs greeted me in the driveway. I left Buddy in the kennel until I made sure the other dogs were back in the house. Buddy's mood was hard to gauge. Usually a dog's tail indicated his mood, but Buddy's tail had been cropped. So had his ears. Cropping prevents ears and tails from being grabbed in a fight.

"Hey, Buddy, you want out?" I asked

His entire body wiggled in anticipation of getting out of the kennel. No problem reading his excitement at the anticipation of freedom. I opened the kennel door, clipped on a leash and he jumped down.

"This is your new home, Buddy," I said. He sniffed Grams, and she petted his head. I led him around the yard and out to the barn. Upon seeing us, Bessie and the horses came to the fence. Buddy stopped and stared. It was his first encounter with something bigger than himself. He didn't bark or growl. With curiosity, he walked to the fence and sniffed.

"Good boy," I said.

We then took him to the fenced-in yard and let him loose. His nose went into overdrive as he smelled the scents of the other dogs, but then he realized he was free and took off running. He ran along the fence, crisscrossed from side to side and ran circles. Then he stopped and stared at us, as if inviting us to play.

"This is your new home," I repeated. He took off running.

"I wonder if he's ever had a yard to run in," Grams said.

After a half hour of freedom, Buddy lay down in the shade of the maple tree. I put the leash on him and took him outside the gate. Grams let the other dogs into the fenced-in area. They came barking to the fence. Buddy pulled on the lead to get closer to them. Through the fence, they all sniffed one another.

"I think they're going to do fine," Grams said. I did too, but I'd still be cautious. My plan was to keep them separated until I felt comfortable letting them be together. Buddy would be staying in Cooper's old room until then.

That night I unpacked the boxes and wondered why I had kept what I did: books I had already read and would never read again, old clothes that were out of style. Grams wasn't impressed with the coat.

"It looks like fox to me," she said as she felt the fur.

"I have a sentimental attachment to it," I explained.

"Aren't memories enough? All this coat represents is death. Maybe Rob would want it," she said.

"I offered the coat to Rob when we divided our stuff during the divorce. He didn't want it."

When I called Cooper that night, I told him about the coat. He wasn't impressed either. "You could donate it to a wildlife rehabber. They give old furs to orphaned babies to snuggle with," he said.

"That's a thought."

I told Cooper that Diesel had been renamed and was spending the night in his old room. He eased my fears by telling me that pit bulls were good dogs, that the owners who trained them to fight were the villains. He felt confident that Buddy had been rehabilitated and would be safe around the other dogs and the cats, but he didn't judge me for being cautious.

I hoped Cooper would bring up what we had discussed the night before: the possibility of having a baby. But he didn't. I'd give him time.

Later that night, I couldn't shake Grams' comments about the coat. I went online and researched fur. It's unlikely that the buyer of a fur coat is aware of how many animals are required to make that single garment: 100 chinchillas or as many as 60 minks are required to make one full-length fur coat and, depending on the type of fox, 10 to 24 may be required. Each year, more than a billion rabbits and 50 million other animals—including foxes, seals, mink and dogs—are raised on fur farms or trapped in the wild and killed for their pelts.

The website, respectforanimals.org, showed cute pictures of individual animals: mink, squirrel, fox, raccoon, dog, bobcat, beaver, chinchilla, lynx, rabbit. Click on a picture and you'd learn how many animals were killed for their fur to make one coat.

For Busia's coat, 10 to 20 foxes died.

Another part of my heart awakened.

On fur farms, wild animals were bred and kept in small cages until they were harvested—that word again. To prevent damage to the fur, their lives were ended by gas or electrocution. Foxes were killed as young as nine months.

Outside my window, a full moon brightened the night landscape. I stared into the familiar but dreamlike scene trying to comprehend the unfairness of life.

As Busia's fur coat rested on my bed, I gently glided my hand over the fur. How could something so soft and lovely be birthed of such cruelty and death? Using my phone, I took a photo of the coat. Telling the dogs to stay, I took the coat downstairs. Quiet, as not to wake Grams, I opened the door and went outside into the moonlit yard. Behind the barn in the farm's pet cemetery, I laid the coat in the grass. I got a shovel and, by moonlight, started digging. Tears streamed down my face. I cried for the young foxes who never knew the feel of grass on their feet, who never knew freedom.

A line from Gordon Lightfoot's song, "The Wreck of the Edmund Fitzgerald," came to mind. "Does anyone know where the love of God goes when the waves turn the minutes to hours?"

Does anyone know where the love of God goes when an animal gets caught in a trap?

Does anyone know where the love of God goes when an animal is born only to live his entire life in a cage?

Does anyone know where the love of God goes when a hunted animal has no chance of escape?

I laid the coat in the grave. "May your souls be at peace," I said. Then I shoveled in the dirt.

Chapter 11

The next morning, I woke to distant gun shots, a reminder that the annual pilgrimage to the woods was about a month away—whitetail deer hunting season. Small game season was underway. There was also a youth hunt for whitetail, but the dates were unknown to me. I hadn't given hunting much thought until my visit to the Great Northern Whitetail Ranch. My mind conjured up a grisly scene with each gunshot that echoed in the distance. At least the wild animals had a chance. Those held captive deserved the same opportunity.

Lying in bed, I had an epiphany ... was God speaking to me? People talk of hearing God's directive, but I have never experienced it. I often wondered if the voice they heard was inside or outside their head. I wondered, too, if drugs had been involved. Who knows? They say God works in mysterious ways, ways I didn't understand.

Anyway, my revelation told me to cut the fences that held animals as prisoners so they could escape. It felt like a command. If not God, who else could it be from? The idea of helping captive animals to escape excited me, and that felt good.

Grams was eating breakfast when I went downstairs. She had let the dogs outside, so I got Buddy and took him for a walk. When I came back in, Grams had a bowl for cereal on the table for me.

"I heard you last night. Did Buddy need to go out?" she asked.

"No," I said as I sat down. Buddy lay down by my feet. By the morning light, my midnight burial sounded off-base, feeling more like a vivid dream than actuality. "I did some reading on fur coats, and decided I didn't want the coat after all."

"What'd you do?"

"Buried it," I said as I poured corn flakes into the bowl and doused them with almond milk.

"What?" she asked, her voice reflecting disbelief. Every now and then, I could still surprise her.

I looked at her. "You heard me right. I gave the foxes a proper burial. Behind the barn. In the pet cemetery."

She smiled and shook her head. "That's the craziest thing you've ever done. Couldn't it have waited until morning?"

"There was a full moon. It felt right."

I took the long way into work that morning. My detour was to scope out another hunting ranch in a neighboring county. As much as I wanted to return to Great Northern Whitetail Ranch, I knew it wouldn't be smart. The owner would surely think of me if vandalism occurred shortly after my tour, and who knows, he may have written down my license plate number or even had cameras somewhere with my face recorded.

My plan was to drive around and look for other possibilities. Hunting ranches were easy to find. They advertised all over the Internet. Plus, they had miles of tall, woven-wire fencing that deer couldn't jump, but it could easily fall prey to bolt cutters.

I had addresses for two farms. The first one was perfect for my plan. A section of the high fence was built near a wooded tract of land where deer could find cover. A two-track lane next to a cornfield provided the perfect place to park. Behind the fence in the distance, I saw a herd of deer.

"I'll be back," I whispered to them.

Although I wasn't late, Cindi was already cleaning kennels when I arrived at work. As we worked, I told her about my weekend, everything except the fur coat.

She invited me to a girls' night out happening that evening. "It's bachelorette party for Carol. She's getting married." Carol was a volunteer at the shelter.

"A bachelorette party on a Monday night?"

"It's a last-minute thing. She's getting married, and Monday was the only night she had free. We're meeting at the Sandbar at six. They have karaoke. We can have dinner, drinks, do some dancing, singing."

"Sounds like fun. I'll be there," I said.

As if it were destiny, the pieces fell into place. After the party at the Sandbar, I'd do my deed. The full moon would provide cover and enough light to work by. Ironically, it was the Harvest Moon.

Chapter 12

While taking Buddy for a walk that evening, I snuck into the garage and borrowed a pair of Gramps' small bolt cutters. They were awkward to work with but would make cutting fences easy and fast. I hid them on the floor of the backseat if my car and covered them with a blanket.

Buddy was adjusting to his new routine. With the other dogs safely in the house, he explored the fenced-in yard. Grams kept an eye on him while I showered and dressed for the evening—black jeans would fit both occasions. I wore a light green blouse for the party but packed a brown T-shirt and an over-sized black jacket for the *afterparty*. I also packed the outfit I wore to the dog fight: a man's hairpiece, a baseball cap and fake glasses. I wondered about binding my chest but decided the big coat would conceal my feminine form. If caught on camera or seen from a distance, I wouldn't look like a woman.

I put Buddy back upstairs in Cooper's room. "You're a good boy. Soon you'll be one of the pack," I cooed to him.

With the disguise in a backpack, I went back downstairs. "I shouldn't be too late but don't wait up for me," I said to Grams as she watched TV with the dogs. She didn't even look up when she told me to have fun.

I stopped at the barn and filled a plastic bag with carrots. This time of year, bags of carrots, apples and corn were sold as deer bait. As much as I hated supporting the hunting industry, the horses loved carrots, so I'd buy a bag to use as treats.

My stomach knotted, a sensation similar to what I felt on the drive to the dog fight. Part anticipation. Part anxiety. Part fear. This time I worked without a safety net. No backup. I didn't want anyone to know what I was doing. It was me and only me. The power of one.

The bachelorette party was a delightful diversion. Close to a dozen women attended, most I didn't know, but they all seemed to know me. I didn't realize my involvement in the dog fight bust had made me a champion among the local animal lovers.

Carol gave me a hug. "I'm honored you came," she said.

"I wouldn't miss it. Congratulations on your marriage."

Cindi ordered two pitchers of beer for the table. The alcohol quenched my nervousness and allowed me to enjoy the evening.

Two people I did know were Dr. Katie and her assistant, Meg. They sat together but at the opposite end of the table from me, so I didn't get to talk to them. Their presence reminded me that I should have called them today about the beagle. I made a mental note to call in the morning.

My ability to sing was the one thing I appreciated inheriting from my mother. When Cindi passed around a song list for karaoke, I glanced it over and selected a Gordon Lightfoot song: "If You Could Read My Mind." I still had Lightfoot music stuck in my head from the drive to Chicago. "If you could read my mind, love, what a tale my thoughts could tell." Fortunately, no one could read my mind that evening.

The Sandbar wasn't busy, which lent itself to an intimate party with beer relaxing everyone's inhibitions. Carol loved to sing and insisted on sharing the stage with whomever dared take the microphone. Like a popstar backup singer, she sang and swayed, but that wasn't always enough. Sometimes she stole center stage and played diva. Other times she shared the mic and chimed in for a duet. Her liveliness surprised me—at the shelter she was quiet and reserved.

When my turn to sing rolled around, Carol motioned me to join her on the stage.

"I love this song," she told the crowd.

I put on a smile and reached for the microphone. Instead of giving it to me, she slipped it into the mic stand and stood directly behind it. She planned on a duet. Everyone clapped and cheered.

All I can say is that for an unrehearsed performance, it went well. Carol knew how to harmonize and didn't stumble over her words or moves. Back in my seat, I kept a close watch on who might be leaving. I didn't want to be the first, but I was anxious to go. When one of the women finally excused herself and said goodnight, I played copycat. Before leaving, I stopped in the bathroom. Meg, who was washing her hands, turned to me.

"Sorry we didn't get a chance to talk. I didn't know you could sing," she said.

"One of my hidden talents. Hey, I forgot to check and see how the beagle's doing."

"He's doing great, but we'll keep him a few more days. I really am interested in adopting him. My husband took our dog," she said.

"That's great," I said. "I mean your wanting to adopt him, not the divorce, unless you're the want who wanted the divorce. Then maybe it's great." I realized I was talking too much and put my finger to my mouth to shush myself. "We'll talk later, okay?"

Meg laughed as she opened the door to leave. "We'll talk later," she repeated.

When I left the bathroom, I headed straight to my car, mentally thanking the party for providing the perfect alibi.

The moon was lifting from the horizon as I drove away from the Sandbar. I pulled into a grocery store parking lot and put on the T-shirt and jacket. I changed my dancing shoes for hikers and put on the wig, cap and glasses. The disguise helped change my inner dialogue too. The apprehension dissipated, and I felt like a superhero ready for battle.

My target was a 30-minute drive away. Believe me when I say 30 minutes is a long time. I sighed in relief when I finally pulled into the two-track and turned off the car. I opened the window and listened. Silence. I turned off the dome light so it wouldn't shine when I opened the door. I removed the bolt cutters and the bag of carrots.

The harvest moon lit the night but created eerie shadows. The cornfield provided perfect cover, but a light breeze rustled the leaves, leaving a menacing Halloween-like atmosphere in its wake. I hurried across the road. There was a slight ditch, but it was dry. I followed the fence-line inland until I was far enough in so the cut fence wouldn't be visible from the road. I set the carrots down and started clipping. Once my eyes grew accustomed to the moonlight, I could almost see as well as I could in daylight. The bolt cutters sliced through the wires like an ax would chop toothpicks. My first cuts were next to a fence pole. Stretching up on my toes, I could reach about six feet high. Then I worked my way across the top and back down again. I thought the bottom of the fence might be buried, but it wasn't. I dragged the cutout section off to the side. The hole was plenty big enough for the deer to get through.

I didn't see any deer. I sprinkled a few carrots inside the enclosure, a few at the fence line and the rest outside in the land of freedom. I waited a few minutes listening. I hoped the deer would smell the carrots and come to investigate. But it remained quiet.

"Here's your chance," I whispered into the night.

Back at the car, I listened for movement within the fenced area. Nothing. Disappointment embraced me. I'm not sure what I had expected. Maybe I thought the herd of deer would be waiting to escape. I longed to see them sneak through my handiwork to safety. Maybe they needed encouragement. I returned to the fence and strained my eyes, but I still didn't see any deer. I headed to the tree line in search of the elusive animals with the intention of coaxing them toward the opening.

The website had said the hunting area was more than a hundred acres, which was a relatively small piece of land that I could easily traverse. Finally, I saw silhouettes of deer in the distance. I circled around the back side of the herd and waved my arms to scare them into moving. They started moving at about the same time a dog began barking somewhere in the direction of the ranch buildings.

"Crap," I said to myself. Without waiting for the deer, I broke into a jog and headed toward the car. Looking over my shoulder, I saw lights come on and heard an engine fire up. "Damn."

The deer stampeded in the wrong direction, but I no longer cared. My intent now was to get back to the car as quickly as possible and leave the area.

I ducked through the hole in the fence, even though there was no need for ducking. I sprinted across the road and quickly settled into the car. Without turning on the headlights, I backed out of the two-track. Why hadn't I backed in? When I was about a mile away and sure no one was tailing me, I switched on the headlights. I berated myself for going inside the enclosure and trying to convince the whitetail to escape. *Stupid. Stupid. Stupid.* Deep breathing helped calm me, but it took the entire drive home before I felt safe.

I no longer felt like a superhero.

All was quiet at home. I tiptoed upstairs and, once inside my room, called Cooper. I told him about the party and the karaoke. I didn't tell him about my escapade, not that he wouldn't approve. I thought he would, but I didn't want him to worry. The late-night mission to free the deer would be my secret.

Chapter 13

By morning, my visit to the hunting preserve felt like nothing more than a dream. That hopeless what-can-I-do feeling had disappeared. In its place was a sense of empowerment, which felt obscenely good. I reclaimed my superhero status.

While Buddy had his turn at freedom in the fenced-in yard, Grams and I ate oatmeal.

"You must have gotten in late," she said.

"We were having fun. Cindi kept buying pitchers of beer. The Sandbar has karaoke, and you know I love to sing."

"Whose party was it?"

"Carol's. She's a volunteer at the shelter. She handles all the calls about feral cats. She's good at convincing people into letting her trap cats, getting them fixed and returning them to where they were caught. I don't think you've met her."

"Does she work with farmers? That's who needs to get their cats fixed."

"I don't think she does any outreach. She just handles the calls when people complain, but that's a good idea. I'll run it by Cindi and see what she thinks." I rinsed my bowl and put it on the counter.

Grams said she'd take care of Buddy so I said goodbye and left for work.

Jason's car was in the parking lot when I arrived. So was Cindi's. They were talking in the office with the door closed, so I started the morning animal-care routine. About a half hour later, Cindi came out.

"Can you come to the office for a minute?" she asked.

"Can I finish this first?" I was almost done with the cat room and wanted to get everyone fed and watered.

"No, we need you now," she said.

Her abruptness made me look at her. "Is everything all right?"

"I hope so," she said.

I closed the cat-room door and followed her to her office. Besides Jason, there was a man in a suit I didn't recognize. I said good morning to Jason.

Good morning," he said. He was all business, as if our cordial friendship had evaporated with the morning fog. "This is William McCarthy, the new sheriff," he said.

I held out my hand. "Pleased to meet you," I said. I hoped I appeared pleased ... and calm. Inside, my stomach was cinching itself tight. All I could think was that I had been caught. Someone had seen me. Then I remembered the bolt cutters were still in my car, on the floor in the backseat covered with a blanket. The empty carrot bag was in there too. How could I have been so stupid as to forget to remove them when I got home last night? I felt cornered. My heart pounded like I was running a marathon.

"Have a seat," Cindi said, as she sat down behind her desk. The two men stood. Intimidating.

I sat down. "What's up? I asked.

"Where were you Saturday?" the sheriff asked.

All three of them stared at me. The question caught me off guard. *Saturday? Why Saturday?* It took me a few seconds to answer.

"I went to Chicago on Saturday to visit my parents. Left around nine in the morning. Stopped in Grand Haven to visit a friend. I came home Sunday night. I picked up a dog at a rescue on the south side of Chicago on the way home."

"Do you have proof?" Sheriff McCarthy asked.

"Like what? I have the dog."

"Gas receipts. Can we get the phone numbers of your parents and your friend? Do you have a number for the rescue?"

"I bought gas in Indiana. I used my credit card but didn't get a receipt, but I'm sure you can check it. I have the numbers on my phone. Can I ask what's going on?"

The sheriff nodded to Jason.

"The guy who owned the trap that the beagle was caught in was found dead Sunday. It looks like he died Saturday night," Jason said. "We don't think it was an accident."

"And you think I did it?" The relief caused me to laugh and to repeat myself. "You really think I killed somebody?"

"No, but we had to check. You were angry with him," Jason said.

"But I didn't want him dead. I just wanted him to get a ticket, to have some kind of consequence for not setting his trap properly."

Although I denied involvement, the sheriff still wanted my credit card number and the phone numbers. I had no choice but to oblige.

When they finished with me, I went back to the cat room. I continued through the force of habit. My mind was far away. What would I have done if they had asked where I had been *last* night? I wondered if any deer had escaped, if the hole in the fence had been discovered. This much I knew: I wouldn't go back to find out. I'd watch the evening news and read the local newspaper. If it had been discovered, it might be newsworthy.

Jason came in when I was almost done. "Sorry about that," he said.

His apology surprised me. "You were just doing your job."

"I didn't think it was you, but the sheriff doesn't know you. He just knows your reputation."

"My reputation?" I stopped and looked at him. "What's my reputation?"

"It's the reason he has his job. Sheriff VanBergen died because you went to the dog fight."

"No," I said. "VanBergen died because he was into dog fighting. He died because he was being blackmailed into keeping his department from investigating it. Sorry I didn't listen to him to not get involved. You knew he wasn't doing his job. You should have done more." I had wanted to say that to Jason for a long time. I knew part of him blamed me for VanBergen's death. I wasn't going to accept the blame.

"I blame you though. You should have told me what you were going to do."

"And what would you have done? I'll tell you what you would have done. You would have stopped me. You would have reported the fight to VanBergen, and he would have told the fight organizers. They would have known they had a snitch, and who knows what would have happened."

"You're right," he said. "Truce?" He held up both hands like he was surrendering.

I nodded yes. "Truce."

"I want to show you something," he said. He pulled out his wallet and took out a folded piece of paper. Unfolding it, he handed it to me.

"What is it?" I asked as I looked at it. I could see that it was a map with X's scribbled in handwriting.

"It's from Joe DeYoung's house."

"Joe DeYoung?"

"You know, the trapper who was murdered."

"What's the map?"

"I'm only guessing, but I think it's his trap line. It was on his kitchen counter. I think we should check the traps. If any animals are caught, we can let them loose."

"How did you get it?"

"I was called in when they saw the written warning I had given him."

"Do they know you took it?"

"Technically, I didn't take it. I just made a copy of it," he said with an impish grin.

"Is this some kind of test? You trying to get me in trouble?" I asked. His friendliness caught me by surprise.

He grabbed the map from my hand. "No, I'm not trying to get you in trouble. I can't believe you even asked that," he said as he refolded the paper and put it back in his wallet.

"You haven't been talking to me. You've been downright cold. Then you ask me to do something that might not be quite legit? What should I think?"

His silence made me think I had gone too far. "I guess I'm still hurt ... mad ... I don't know. I'm trying to get past it. As far as being legit, I don't know why it wouldn't be. Do you want to help or not?" When I didn't answer right away, he turned to leave.

"Wait a minute. Sorry, I need to think," I said. He stopped without saying anything and waited. I wanted to go. I wanted to trust him. I wanted our friendship restored. "I'll go. What time were you thinking?" I asked.

"As soon as possible. What do you have going on today?"

"Looks like I'm helping you."

Chapter 14

Jason had already studied the map and thought he knew where the traps might be located.

"What do you mean, you think you know?" I asked as we worked together readying the dog kennels for the day. I poured water into bowls and dished out kibble. He picked up poop and mopped where needed.

"The map covers a small piece of land with a creek that I matched with a map of the county, but I could be wrong."

I stood up and did a back stretch. "What you're saying is that we might be bushwhacking the rest of the day. Is this payback time?"

We used to tease each other about my owing him big-time. A few months back, when I discovered the dog fighters' dumping ground for the corpses of the defeated dogs and bait animals, I asked Jason for assistance. We inventoried the bodies and then buried them, quite a gruesome undertaking. Later I talked him into helping me dig up the carcasses to scan them for microchips, which was even more horrific. The stench stayed with me for days. Jason blamed me for getting him involved in the unpleasant task. I reminded him that helping me was part of his job. Asking about payback was meant as banter, but he took it seriously.

"I hope not. I'm hoping we find empty traps, not dead or dying animals," he said.

For some reason, I assumed we would find empty traps. Now I regretted agreeing to help. What would be worse to find— injured animals or dead animals? But then I remembered what the salesman at the sports store had said: leg-hold traps were not designed to kill, just to hold.

With two of us working, it didn't take long to finish taking care of the shelter dogs, who were anxious for a reprieve from their cages. Volunteers were scheduled to come midmorning to walk and give them attention. For now, clean cages, food and water would have to do.

"If we're going to be hiking in the woods, I need better shoes and bug spray," I told Jason. "I'm going to run home and change."

"I'll follow you and drive from there," Jason said.

At the house, Grams was walking Buddy, so Jason got to meet the former fighter.

"We're still keeping him separated from the other dogs, but he's doing good," I said.

Jason slowly approached Buddy and stroked his head, and then his body. When Jason quit, Buddy rubbed his head on Jason's leg as if asking for more attention.

"He's a sweetie. His name fits," he said as he gave Buddy more back rubs.

"Better than Diesel, for sure," I said. I excused myself and went and changed my shoes and grabbed an old jacket. In a small backpack, I packed bug spray, apples, granola bars and water.

"Be careful," Grams said. Jason must have told her what we were doing.

According to Jason, the area we were going to was about five miles from Joe's house. On the drive, he asked about my weekend in Chicago. I told him about the fire and how Rocky planned on continuing his work. We were talking, and it felt good.

Jason turned onto a seasonal gravel road that followed alongside a creek. When he thought we were getting close, he pulled off into what looked like a parking spot. Tire tracks could be seen in the soft mix of dirt and dead leaves.

"Maybe they're Joe's tracks," Jason said.

I pulled on the backpack, and Jason grabbed a canvas bag from the back of his truck.

"What's the plan?" I asked.

"We collect the traps. Let's hope they're empty. If they're not, we'll release the animals if they aren't hurt too bad. If they are ... we'll play it by ear."

"Do you know what he was trapping?" I asked.

"I'm guessing raccoons. The traps are close to the water. Raccoons like water."

According to the map, all six traps were along the creek. That would help, but locating them was going to be like looking for the proverbial needle in a haystack. And like the needle, the traps had the potential to cause pain.

"They're too small for a human foot to get caught in," Jason reassured me.

We spread out to cover more ground. Jason suggested we use sticks to poke into piles of leaves that may have been used to cover the telltale metal.

The water in the small creek cascaded over rocks and fallen trees, making a gentle sound. We climbed over logs, through prickly underbrush and ducked under low-hanging branches, all the time prodding unnatural-looking mounds with our walking sticks.

Jason found the first trap. The end of two logs had been placed together to form a V. Branches covered the logs, creating a cubby hole. Inside, the trap covered with leaves waited for its victim. Jason pulled the branches off and found a pile of marshmallows used as bait. Using a stick, Jason poked the trap and it slammed closed. He removed the stick, and unchained the trap from the log.

"One down, five to go," he said. He took a minute to show me how the trap worked. There were levers on each side of the trap's jaws. When the levers were pressed down, the jaws opened. "It takes a lot of pressure," he said. "It'll be a trick to do it with a wild animal in it."

We continued to follow the creek. At least now we had an idea of what we were looking for. The noise of rustling leaves led us to the second trap. A huge raccoon strained to get away from us, but he couldn't get far, for his front leg was held fast in the trap. He struggled violently to get free.

Jason emptied the canvas bag. "I'm going to cover him with the bag. Then you're going to hold him while I open the trap," he said.

All I could do was nod in agreement. The raccoon quit struggling when we got close, but his eyes followed our every move. He knew he couldn't escape. Jason opened the bag, dropped it over the scared animal and, with one foot, held one side of the bag securely to the ground. He cinched the bag tight with only the raccoon's foot exposed.

"Put your foot next to mine and your hand next to mine," he instructed. I moved in and used my weight to hold the covered raccoon in place. "When his leg is freed, he might start to fight. If he does, let him go. He's going to run," Jason said.

It was awkward, my holding the bag and Jason trying to get an arm on each side of the animal to get to the levers.

"Here goes," he said. I felt his body tense as he pushed down. "He should be free," Jason said. "I can't hold it very long. See if you can get him to go." As soon as I shifted my weight so I could move the canvas, the raccoon bolted. I lost my balance and tumbled into Jason, knocking him down.

"Well, that worked just fine," Jason exclaimed, laughing. He dusted dirt and leaves from his pants when he got up.

I looked for the raccoon, but he was gone. "I sure hope he's okay," I said.

"He'll be limping for a few days. I got a good look at his leg, and it didn't look bad," Jason said. He pulled the stake out of the ground that had secured the trap and placed it in the bag along with the traps.

The next two traps were empty, but we weren't so lucky with the last two. One held a smaller raccoon. Using the same technique, we had him free in minutes, this time without tipping over. The last trap had an opossum. He was subdued and didn't struggle like the raccoons had.

"Is he okay?" I asked.

"I think so," Jason said as he took the traps out of the bag so we could use the bag to cover the scared boy. The opossum was much easier to deal with, except he didn't run once we had him free.

"Let's walk away and give him a few moments," Jason said. We backed up and then turned and pretended to leave. We waited ten minutes and returned. Mr. Opossum was nowhere to be seen. We collected all the traps and headed back to the truck.

"Good thing you found the map," I said. "They would have

died a horrible death if we hadn't helped."

"I can see why you don't like trapping," Jason admitted. "It definitely felt good setting them free."

When I got home that night, I returned the bolt cutters to the garage. Over dinner I told Grams about the afternoon's accomplishments. I echoed Jason's sentiment. "It felt really good to set them free," I said.

When she settled in to watch TV, I called Cooper and told him about releasing the animals from the traps.

"You're almost a member of the Save Five Club," he said.

He had to explain the club to me again. It was a takeoff on the big-game hunters' African Big Five, which were the five most difficult animals in Africa to hunt: the lion, elephant, Cape buffalo, leopard and rhinoceros. To be a member of the Animal Liberation League's Save Five Club, you had to rescue an animal from a factory farm, a fur farm, from hunting, a research lab and an animal from the entertainment industry, like a circus, zoo or rodeo.

I had rescued Kal, a mouse, from a lab. I also saved a dairy cow from slaughter—Bessie. I saved Buddy from dog fighting.

"Some people consider that entertainment," Cooper had said. "But there's something wrong with people who enjoy watching dogs kill each other."

Now I had helped save the raccoons and opossum.

"They weren't from a fur farm, but they would have been killed, skinned and their fur used for fashion. All you have to do is save an animal from being hunted," Cooper concluded.

I thought of the deer, but didn't tell Cooper that I might have already accomplished saving an animal from being hunted.

Chapter 15

Our cow Bessie came from a dairy farm. When she no longer produced the amount of milk the farm owner expected, he sent her to slaughter. The truck carrying Bessie and other cows to their final destiny had overturned. Several cows died in the accident, but not Bessie. She escaped unharmed and disappeared into the nearby woods. I spent days trying to catch her but, as she had experienced her first taste of freedom, she steered clear of me. When Jason and I finally caught her, I couldn't bring myself to hand her over to the dairy farmer who owned her. I knew her destiny was slaughter. Ground beef for fast-food burgers.

Looking back, I realized that Bessie had caused my awakening toward milk, cheese and ice cream. Dairy no longer tasted the same. Instead of a delectable indulgence, it became a guilty pleasure, and then it morphed into a painful reminder that somewhere a calf had been stolen from his mother.

"You're not going back to him," I recalled whispering to Bessie. Instead of delivering her to the farmer, I had her trucked to Grams' farm.

Instead of a cow, Mr. Dairy Farmer got a bill for my time. He called and complained. He yelled. He refused to pay. He said the bill was more than the damn cow was worth. I knew that. That's why I mailed him the invoice. When he didn't pay to claim Bessie in 30 days, she became the property of the county—more specifically, the shelter owned her. When no one adopted her, I did.

When Bessie first arrived at the farm, Grams insisted she be checked by a veterinarian. Dr. Livingston called Bessie a spent dairy cow who was only good for beef. I knew that. He guessed she was about six years old—old for a cow used at an industrial dairy; young for a cow whose natural lifespan could be upwards of 20 years. Doc Livingston also told us that Bessie had a secret. She was pregnant.

"They must have run the numbers and decided her milk didn't justify feed. Younger cows produce better," he explained.

I remember listening to him and being dumbfounded all over again. When I had visited Clover Dairy, where Bessie had been enslaved, I learned about the milk industry. Apparently, I had blocked some of the horrendous details from my mind. Who wants to know the brutal facts of where their food comes from? When dunking a chocolate-chip cookie into a cold glass of milk, who wants to think of the calf deprived of his mother's milk?

As a city girl, I hadn't known a cow had to give birth to produce milk. Made sense when I thought about it. I also remember being horrified to learn that calves were taken from their mothers shortly after birth.

That's when I quit drinking milk. Quit eating cheese. Quit eating ice cream until I discovered dairy-free ice cream.

As Bessie's delivery day neared, we began hovering over her like expectant grandparents. There wasn't a specific due date, but Doc Livingston had given us his best guess. As Bessie's bulging sides grew, our watch intensified.

To my surprise, when I went to do chores in the morning, Bessie was no longer big, but I didn't see a calf. She was munching on grain as she did every other day. I sprinted to the house shouting, "Grams, I think Bessie had her baby, but I don't know where it is!"

She met me on the porch. "What? Bessie had her baby?"

"Looks like it to me, but the calf's not with her."

We hurried to the barn. As usual, Bessie was standing at the trough by the horses.

"She definitely gave birth," Grams remarked after seeing Bessie's thin sides.

We opened the gate and went into the pasture. "Let's take a walk and see what we can find," Grams said. We headed to the grove of trees where Bessie often snoozed in the shade.

As we walked, Grams nudged me and tilted her head,

indicating that I should look behind us. Bessie had left her food and was following us. As we got closer to the trees, she broke into a trot and ran in front of us. Then she stopped and turned. She put her head down and stared at us as if daring us to come closer.

We stopped—I had learned long ago not to mess with a protective mother.

"She thinks we're here to take her calf," Grams said. "She's never been allowed to keep her baby."

"What should we do?"

"Let's leave her alone." We backed up then, keeping an eye on Bessie. When we felt safe, we turned and made our way back to the barn. From there, we watched as Bessie went into the trees. A tiny black and white calf, looking like a mini-Bessie, came out to meet her.

"She's going to keep this calf," Grams whispered. Her soft voice surprised me. Tears rolled down her checks as she watched the newborn suckle.

A feeling of satisfaction washed over me. Saving one cow and letting her be a mother wasn't much in the big industry of factory farming, but it felt good.

Distant gunshots broke the tranquil moment.

"Damn hunters," Grams growled.

The gunshots reminded me of my quest to free deer from canned hunts.

Chapter 16

In doing research on hunting preserves, one thing irritated me more than the others: the name Whitey's Whitetail Sanctuary. A sanctuary was meant to be a place of safety, a refuge, not a place of death. According to the website, every hunt came with a guarantee and a guide. The guide knew which animal you had paid for and knew the herd's routine. The way I saw it, one of Whitey's hunts wouldn't be a hunt at all; it would be target practice.

On Google maps, I saw several buildings but couldn't make out all the fence lines, as forests obscured the view.

Whitey's was less than an hour's drive away, its proximity making it my next mark. I'd do a drive-by in the morning to scope out possible parking places, and then return later. Grams had a garden-club meeting in the evening, so she wouldn't be home expecting me for dinner.

Before leaving for work, I loaded my disguise and bolt cutters in the car. After saying goodbye to Grams, I headed east. The route was in my head. I didn't want any telltale evidence on my phone, not that I didn't worry about the searches done on my home computer. I deleted any revealing signs, but no doubt they could be found by someone who knew how to look. In my mind, the risk was worth it.

One thing about hunting preserves is that they are usually quite rural and have miles of fencing, which creates plenty of opportunities for someone with illicit ideas. I drove the roads twice around the preserve looking for the best spot to park. There was only one area where I could see the animals. Unfortunately, it was close to the main road where I would run the risk of being seen. Plus, the deer could be hit in the road. I chose a place on

69

the isolated backside of the preserve where woods provided cover. Baiting and herding would be necessary.

When I got to the shelter, I cleaned kennels and walked dogs. There were adoption applications to review and the never-ending pile of paperwork, emails and phone calls.

After lunch, I got a call from Meg at Dr. Johnson's office. "He barged in here and demanded that we give him his dog," she said in a voice louder than normal.

Who?" I asked. I couldn't figure out what she was talking about.

"Stanley Jones, the owner of the beagle with the amputated leg."

"Oh. He told me he didn't want the dog."

"He must have changed his mind. We couldn't stop him. We tried. He bullied his way in and took the beagle."

"He what?"

"He went in the back and carried the dog out. We told him he had a bill to pay. He told us he "'ain't paying no damn bill.' We didn't argue. He was scary."

"I'm sorry. I'll take care of it. How was Buster doing? Was he ready to be released?"

"He was doing okay, but the bandage needs to be changed and the incision kept clean."

"Okay, I'll go see him tomorrow and let you know what I find out." I didn't relish the idea of confronting Stanley, but I couldn't let him get away with taking his dog and not paying the bill.

Jason stopped by the shelter close to quitting time when I was almost finished tucking in the animals for the night.

"What's up?" I asked.

He had picked up a stray dog and was admitting it to quarantine. I helped him with the paperwork and getting the scared pup settled in his kennel.

"Did they figure out who killed the trapper yet?" I asked when he came into the office.

"Not that I've heard," he said.

I told him about Stanley Jones barging into the vet's office and taking his dog. "I need to go out there tomorrow. Can you go with? He might respond better to a guy," I said.

"Sure. What time?"

"In the morning. Whenever you're free. I'll be here."

After Jason left, I went into town. The plan was to be at Whitey's at dusk. I had enough time to grab a veggie burrito before making the drive.

The evening sky with its streaks of red, purple and orange smoldered in my rearview mirror. Rippled clouds provided the type of view that brought people to the big lake to take in the performance of the sun settling into the water.

For me, the fading light was a signal to get clipping. I backed the car into a trail in the woods that provided perfect cover. The nearest house was more than a mile away. I slipped on the hair piece, fake glasses and shabby jacket. I grabbed the cutters and bag of carrots. My previous experience brought speed and technique—let the fence wire slide all the way into the throat of the cutter. Apply a steady pressure until the release, which came with the cut. Slip in the next wire and repeat. After the section of fencing was completely free, I pulled it inside the enclosure and dragged it off to the side. I dumped a few carrots outside the fence. The rest I dropped at intervals to create a trail into the field. Then I went in search of the herd. It didn't take long to find them. I'm guessing they heard me and were coming to investigate. So much for being wild. They were used to humans providing food.

I backed off when they got close. When the first one discovered the carrots, I knew it was time to go. I made my way back to the car and watched. My heart skipped a beat with happiness as the first deer made its way outside the fence. He was magnificent: huge, with antlers like I had never seen before. I wondered if he would have a chance on the outside. With such a stunning rack, I knew the odds of his survival were low no matter where he was, but his chance of living was higher with more land to roam.

"Be safe," I whispered.

Chapter 17

Jason was at the shelter when I arrived the next morning. This time I remembered to remove all evidence from my car before heading to work.

"Good morning. I'm almost ready to go see Stanley," he said. He had made a pot of coffee and was sitting in the breakroom sipping a cup of the hot brew. "I brought us a treat," he said pointing to a tray of raspberry Danish that sat on the table with a piece missing.

I poured myself a cup of coffee and served myself a slice of the morning sweet.

"Carol is here with a new volunteer, so the animals are set," he said.

"I love new volunteers. I need to go meet her. Give me a minute," I said. I went in the back and introduced myself. Her name was Bobbie, and she was a friend of Carol's.

"Carol's been bugging me to come and help. The time was finally right," she said.

"Thank you. Thank you. Thank you," I said. "We wouldn't survive without volunteers." I offered coffee and Danish, courtesy of Jason, when they were ready for a break.

Back in the breakroom, Jason was rinsing his coffee cup. "Let's do it," I said taking my coffee and cake with me.

In his truck, Jason asked for the game plan.

"Let's swing by Dr. Katie's office and pick up an updated invoice," I said. "We can give him a choice: pay or give us the dog back." I rolled the window down to let in the unseasonably warm autumn air.

Jason turned on a rock station as we sped down the road.

"Isn't making him pay the bill a little harsh? Odds are he doesn't have the money to pay."

"It's his attitude that bugs me. If he showed an ounce of compassion or offered to pay part of the bill, I'd be more forgiving."

"You're too involved. Will you let me do the talking?"

"Sure, handle it your way."

Meg was happy to get us the invoice for Buster. While she pulled it up on the computer to print, she gave us a minute-by-minute description of Stanley's visit.

"He stormed in here demanding his dog. I couldn't figure out what he was talking about. Then he started swearing about us cutting his dog's leg off. By then he had pushed past me and headed toward the back."

"Were there other people here?" I asked.

"A couple. They just watched. They weren't going to confront him, and I don't blame them."

"I didn't expect them to—" Meg didn't let me finish my thought.

"I followed him to the back. He looked around, and when he saw Buster, he picked him up. I told him he needed to pay the bill."

"What did he say to that?"

"He snorted and said 'make me.' I told him the bandage needed to be changed, and we needed to do a follow up visit."

"I'm sure that won't happen," I said.

"He was such a nice dog. I hate that he's got such an ass for an owner," she said.

"We'll see what we can do," Jason said. "We're heading over there right now."

Meg folded the bill, put it into an envelope and handed it to me.

Stanley lived on the north side of the county. The first time I had gone to his place, I didn't have time to look around. Our brief encounter in his driveway had taken me by surprise, and all I recalled was Stanley's nasty behavior. With Jason driving, I had time to inspect Stanley's home as we approached. It was so small it looked like it would fit inside a two-stall garage. At one time, it had been white, but time had taken advantage of the protective covering, giving the humble abode a look of weathered gray with a tinge of flaked and peeling paint.

"It must be one of the original houses in the county," Jason said, as he drove into the driveway.

The grass was knee high and branches cluttered the yard. A tired-looking snowmobile sat next to the house. An unattached garage in the side yard looked as run down as the house. Behind the house was a small weathered barn.

"His truck isn't here. He must not be home," I said as we got out.

We knocked on the door, and no one answered, but the knocking aroused his dogs who started to howl. The distinct beagle bark came from the direction of the barn.

"Let's see if Buster is in there," I said.

"We shouldn't," Jason said as he followed me behind the house. The back of the house was hidden by piles of stuff: rough sawn pallets, stacks of fire wood, a push lawn mower that looked like it belonged in a museum and a wooden rocking chair. Grass worn down to dirt in front of the rocker suggested it was Stanley's hangout.

Next to the barn was a fenced-in yard containing a flock of about a dozen chickens scratching and pecking at the ground. They ignored us and the dogs who were howling and running back and forth by the fence. One of the dogs was missing a leg. The bandage was off, but the wound looked healed and somewhat clean. The dogs looked healthy, and their friendliness indicated they were well cared for and maybe even loved. Buster recognized me and quieted down when I reached through the fence to greet him.

"I think we should take him and leave the bill," I said as I squatted down and petted Buster. The other dogs nosed their way to my hand and accepted backrubs. "I'll leave my card and ask him to call."

Jason wasn't keen on the idea but relented.

So that's what I did. I scribbled my name and number on the back of a shelter business card and wrote that we had confiscated the beagle. "Please call," I had added. Buster's tail wagged as

I picked him up, careful not to get close to where his leg was missing.

"Are you going to take him back to Dr. Katie's clinic?" Jason asked as we settled in the truck.

Holding Buster on my lap, I told him no, that I thought taking him home would be safer for him. "Let's keep Dr. Katie and her staff out of this. He can come to the shelter and talk to me."

Instead of going to the shelter, Jason drove to the farm. We set Buster up in a spare stall in the barn. Fresh straw gave him a clean place to sleep. I gave him food and water. Grams wasn't home, so I left her a note about the temporary visitor.

Chapter 18

Taking Buster from Stanley Jones' backyard was one of the biggest mistakes of my life. Maybe the biggest. But how was I to know? I should have listened to Jason. Why was I so bullheaded? The consequences of that decision will haunt me forever.

When I got home from work the night after we rescued Buster, the beagle was snoozing in his stall. "Buster," I called. He was one of those dogs who was always happy. Despite losing a leg, he danced about in anticipation of attention. I plopped my butt down in the straw, and he came and rested his head in my lap.

"You're such a good boy," I told him as I rubbed his back. He rolled over onto his back so his belly could be scratched too.

"Is Stanley good to you? Do you want to go back and live with him?" I wished animals could answer my questions. Sometimes it was hard to know what was best. Maybe Stanley was just a gruff old man who needed understanding. Maybe.

Buster's wound looked fine: no discoloration, no swelling. I clipped a leash to his collar and took him for a short walk. Missing a leg didn't hinder him. He sniffed the ground, the bushes, the trees and took in the scents of all the dogs. He stayed with me while I fed the barn cats and horses. Bessie was still out under the trees. I called her. She looked but didn't budge. She'd rather miss dinner than risk losing her baby.

"Your baby is safe here," I shouted to her. She didn't answer me either.

Grams had gathered the last of the veggies from her garden and made a harvest stew for dinner. The stew was an annual tradition to celebrate the end of the growing season. Winter lurked in our future, but for now the fall weather hung on and gave us warm sunny days and vibrant red and yellow vistas.

After dinner, we sat together on the porch swing sipping red wine. There wouldn't be many such nights left to enjoy the swing. We often spent our evenings swinging and chatting. Buster dominated our conversation. Grams thought he should go back to his owner.

"The dog's been well cared for. What if the guy can't afford to pay the bill? He's probably paid property taxes in this county his entire life. Let the county pick up the tab," she said.

"You're right," I said. "When he calls tomorrow, I'll tell him I'll drop the dog off."

When I talked to Cooper that night, he felt the same way. "There's a shortage of homes for shelter dogs. Why adopt this dog out when he already has an owner? It wasn't his fault the dog got caught in a trap."

In my mind it was settled. Buster would go back to Stanley. But Stanley never called me the next day. Instead, Jason called.

"You need to lock the shelter and get everyone out," he shouted.

"What? Why? What's going on?"

"I'm at Dr. Katie's. There's no time to sugar coat it. Dr. Katie is dead. So is Meg. They've been shot. Someone saw a black pickup. I'm guessing it's Stanley Jones. If it was him, he's likely looking for you. You need to leave. Do it. Lock the doors and leave." There was an urgency in Jason's voice that I'd never heard before.

"Okay, okay. We're leaving."

I turned off my computer, locked the front door and flipped the open sign to closed. Cindi was the only other person at the shelter. I told her what Jason had said.

"He wants us out of here. He thinks Stanley is on his way," I said speaking twice as fast as normal. "Where do we go?" Then I thought of Grams. She was home alone. If Stanley knew where I lived, he might go there. "I'm going home. Grams is alone," I said. Cindi, who knew Grams well, said she'd follow me, and we'd wait it out together at the farm.

We peeked out the front window looking for the black pickup. The parking lot was empty so we snuck out the back door and ran to our cars. There were no vehicles in sight as we left.

I'd be lying if I said I didn't speed on the way home. I prayed Grams was okay. I berated myself for taking Buster. Jason had been right. Why didn't I listen to him? There was a county police car in the yard when I pulled in. My heart froze. A deputy stood on the back porch. I ran to him.

"Where's Grams," I yelled.

He held up his hands to stop me. "She's in the house. She's fine. Jason sent me here to guard her," he said.

I collapsed onto the porch. Cindi wrapped her arm around me and helped me to stand.

"She's okay," Cindi whispered.

The door opened and Grams came out. "Jason told me what happened," she said. She hugged me, and I didn't want to let her go. We finally went into the house. The deputy provided a sense of security.

A shotgun pointing at the back door lay on the kitchen table. "Tom believed in his second amendment rights," Grams said. Tom—or Gramps to me—was her late husband, my grandfather. He had taught me how to safely handle a gun and how to shoot. But since he died, we hadn't needed to get the shotgun out of the gun cabinet.

Grams poured me a drink. "Leftover from Tom," she said. "He liked his whiskey."

I shook my head no. "I need a clear head," I said. "If he comes, I can't be lightheaded."

"If he comes, you aren't going to see him," Grams said. "He'll be arrested. Or shot." She put the whiskey away and made a pot of coffee.

We sat at the kitchen table, waiting.

Chapter 19

We waited all day. Stanley never showed up. The entire county was looking for him. Soon the entire state was looking for him. He had disappeared.

Another deputy relieved the first cop and said he'd be there until morning. We wanted to go back to the shelter to care for the animals, but Jason said no. He would take care of everything. Cindi was escorted home to take care of her pets, and then she came back to spend the night. She brought her black lab, Jethro, with her.

"I can't believe he'd shoot two people over a dog," I said as we sat around the kitchen table. The guilt was overwhelming.

"You didn't know he was unhinged," Grams said. "If you had known, you would have handled it differently."

She was right, but the sympathetic words didn't diminish my anguish. "How can someone point a gun at a person and pull the trigger?" I found the concept as foreign as the idea of pointing a gun at an animal and pulling the trigger.

"Anyone in their right mind couldn't," Cindi said. "He's obviously sick."

Our conversation was sprinkled with long bouts of silence. What could be said? We speculated where Stanley could be. Had he realized he had gone too far? Was he running? Hiding?

"He could disappear into the Manistee Forest and never be found. He has the skills to live off the land," Grams said.

"Where does that leave us? Confined to the house until they find him?" I asked. Sooner or later, we would have to return to our everyday life. The thought of being locked in the house spurred me to go outside. "I'm going to the barn."

"We'll go with you," Cindi said. She pushed her chair back and stood.

"Good idea," Grams said.

I got Buddy from Cooper's room. So far, he was doing fine. When the other dogs ran lose, I kept him on a leash. The gang did a lot of sniffing but eventually lost interest in him.

"Come on guys, we're going out," I said. The five dogs didn't need to be told. They read my mind and were two steps ahead of me. Jethro joined right in.

The deputy was sitting in his car. We reminded him he was welcomed to come in the house. He said he would be in later. We asked if it was okay to go to the barn. He gave his permission and said he'd watch us.

"I don't think anyone would dare do anything with that rowdy pack with you," he said. Elvis, Sinatra, Cody, Blue, Shadow and Jethro ran high-speed around the yard, occasionally stopping to sniff or pee. Buddy wanted to join them.

"Should I let him go?" I asked Grams and Cindi. Grams nodded yes. I unclipped the leash. "Be good or you'll be back on the leash," I warned. He took off running to join the group. They greeted him with barks, and then they were all zooming around the yard again.

"Looks like he's doing okay," Grams said.

I nodded. For Mike's sake, I hoped Buddy would fit in. I thought Mike would be pleased to know the dog he gave his life for was living a good life just being a dog. No more fighting. Wherever Mike was, I hoped he knew.

Leaving the dogs outside, I went in to check Buster. For the first time, the darkness of the barn had an eerie feel. Stanley had me spooked. Buster heard me and started barking. He most likely heard the other dogs and wanted out of solitary confinement.

"Soon you'll be able to join them," I said. He looked and acted fine. I cleaned up his stall and gave him some kibble and fresh water. He needed exercise, but I didn't want to take him out while the other dogs were loose.

Grams had gone to feed the horses. Bessie joined them, but she still wasn't sharing her calf with us. Grams explained the situation to Cindi.

"Shouldn't we go out and see if the calf is okay?" I asked Grams.

"He's okay. I've seen him twice. We'll give her a couple more days. If she doesn't bring him up, I'll go out and check on him. Maybe that will give her the confidence to bring him around."

Getting out of the house had been a good distraction. When we returned to our confinement, Grams warmed up leftover harvest stew. Although I appreciated the spicy aroma, I had no interest in eating.

The shooting was the top story on the six o'clock news. "Two dead at veterinary clinic." Details hadn't been released, but Stanley Jones was a person of interest, and the public was asked to watch for him and his black pickup. He was considered armed and dangerous.

Jason stopped by after dinner. He didn't have anything new to report. He just wanted to assure us he had taken care of the shelter animals and would do so again in the morning.

"Until he's found, I want you here with protection," he said.

I was subdued with guilt. "Whatever you say," I said. He didn't answer. I knew what he was thinking—why hadn't I listened to him yesterday? Then none of this would have happened. His silence amplified the guilt. Anger or "I told you so" would have been better than silence. He didn't stay long.

Grams made a pot of coffee for the deputy. We left all the lights on in the downstairs when we went to bed. I called Cooper. As I recounted the day's events, I broke into sobs.

"I can't believe this is happening," I said, wiping tears from my face. He hadn't understood what I said, so I had to repeat the telling. "They're dead because of me."

Chapter 20

After talking to Cooper, I took a hot bath, hoping the warmth would help me sleep. It didn't. Ebony, the black cat who adopted me when I investigated the cat-hoarding situation, wouldn't leave me alone. She knew I needed a friend. While I soaked in the bath, she snoozed on the bathmat.

After my bath, I tried to read but couldn't concentrate. Online, I searched for stories about the shooting and re-watched the newscast about the incident. The local newspaper had an article, but it didn't have any new information. The whole time Ebony sat on my lap.

Shortly after midnight, I resorted to a sleeping pill. Why hadn't I taken one earlier? Even with the pill, my sleep was restless. Memories of Dr. Katie and Meg wouldn't leave me alone. Meg was just about to start a new life. A life as a single woman. And just like that, it was over. I recalled telling her that things would get better. They should have, but because of me she was dead. Guilt tormented me. My sleep was fragmented with nightmares of guns, scraggly old men, screams and dead bodies.

A sleeping-pill-induced grogginess stayed with me throughout the morning. I overpowered it with coffee, but still felt dazed. Cindi felt a need to go home after breakfast, and Jason approved. He asked that we wait at least another day before going back to the shelter. A different deputy was on duty. His presence in the house was awkward and yet comforting.

Midafternoon Jason called with news. Stanley had been located. He was in the Upper Peninsula and had been there since the afternoon of the day he picked up Buster. He knew nothing about the shooting. A trooper from the State Police had spotted his truck and verified his story.

"A neighbor of his was feeding his dogs and took your note," Jason said. "He told us Stanley was in the U.P."

I no longer heard Jason as I grasped what he was telling me. *Dr. Katie and Meg hadn't been killed by Stanley Jones. I wasn't responsible for their deaths.*

"Alison, are you still there? Alison?"

His repeat of my name broke through my thoughts. "Yes, I'm here. Sorry. I'm just so relieved it wasn't my fault."

Grams was listening and nudged me to tell her what was happening. I asked Jason to hold on while I told her his news. When I returned, he said they had another suspect.

"We think it was Meg's husband. He's being questioned right now."

"You're kidding me. Her husband? I knew she was going through a divorce, but I didn't know why. She never gave any indication she was scared of him."

Jason ended by telling me that I could get back to work. He was going to call Cindi next. I asked that he tell her I'd be heading to the shelter within minutes.

On the way in, I called Carol and asked if she could come help walk the dogs. I knew they'd be antsy after being caged with minimum care. She was happy to oblige.

I also called and left Cooper a message. He'd be at work, but I wanted him to know about the new development. After crying on the phone to him last night, I knew he'd be worried and concerned.

It felt good to be out of the house. What felt even better was the relief of not feeling responsible for the deaths of my friends, but the murders were still a tragedy. Dr. Katie had done all the veterinarian work for the shelter. She would be missed.

Cindi greeted me with a hug. "I bet you're relieved," she said.

I nodded. "I am, but it's still so sad. I'll never understand why men kill their wives. Why can't they just let them go?"

Cindi didn't have an answer. "I don't know," she said.

Carol came in. She knew the shelter's closing was related to the shooting, but she wasn't aware of all the details. I filled her in with what I thought was prudent. She had known Dr. Katie and Meg, having helped transport animals from the shelter to the clinic for spay/neuter surgeries.

"I used her for my own pets, too," she said.

The animals were the first order of business. Cindi took care of the cats while Carol and I cleaned kennels and fed, watered and walked the dogs. Work felt good.

Chapter 21

After the animals were taken care of, I turned my attention to voice mail. There were 24 messages. Ironically, one was from Stanley's neighbor telling me that Stanley was on a trip up north and would get my message when he got back. I returned the call and asked the neighbor to tell Stanley that I would bring the beagle back to him when the dog was healed. "It'll be a couple weeks. Tell him he won't have to pay the vet bill. We'll take care of it," I said.

Cindi and I worked into the early evening, returning phone calls and answering emails. I should have accessed the emails from home but, to be honest, the thought never crossed my mind.

When I got home that night, Grams was sitting at the kitchen table reading the newspaper. She pushed it over to me.

"Is that you?" she asked pointing to a picture.

My first thought was that she was reading something about the shooting, but what picture would they have printed? And why? I sat down and looked at the photo. I gasped and momentarily held my breath. It was me. Me wearing the man's hairpiece, fake glasses and old coat. I recognized the location: Whitey's Whitetail Sanctuary. I was near the fence with bolt cutters in my hand. The story that accompanied the grainy black-and-white photograph was about someone cutting fences at hunting preserves, allowing whitetail deer to escape. They called it vandalism. Owners of two other preserves reported similar incidents.

I sat in stunned silence.

"It is you, isn't it?" Grams asked as she stood up. "I knew it. I recognized that getup. What were you thinking?" Her voice grew louder as she spoke. Grams had never yelled at me before. "Just tell me why."

"They're canned hunts. The deer aren't scared of humans and have no escape. The hunts are guaranteed. It's wrong. I had to do something," I said trying to defend my actions.

"You broke the law. You know better than that. It was a stupid thing to do."

There wasn't anything I could say to appease her, so I stayed quiet. I noticed the dogs had all left the room. Too bad I couldn't join them.

"At least you were smart enough to wear a disguise. I doubt if anyone will recognize you with the quality of the photo being so bad. You have to promise me you won't do it again. Does anyone else know about this? Cooper?"

"No one knows. Not even Cooper. I promise I won't do it again." She made me feel like a child being reprimanded. I didn't appreciate it.

"Do you realize what could happen? You could go to jail. Or have to pay a fine. Paying an attorney would break us!" she shouted.

"I got it," I said as I stood up and faced her. "I got it. I won't do it again. What more do you want?"

She stared at me for what seemed minutes but was probably only seconds. "I think you need to leave until the story dies down," she said.

"Leave? And go where? Won't people find it suspicious if I leave town?" I couldn't believe she was suggesting such a thing. Like I should go into hiding.

"No, with the shooting we can say you needed a break. It would be believable."

"Okay, where do I go?" Sara popped into my mind. So did Cooper. Without giving Grams a chance to answer, I suggested going to Grand Haven to visit Sara. She thought it was a good idea.

When I called Cooper that night, I told him I was thinking of taking a few days off. To my surprise, he suggested we go somewhere together.

"How are the colors in Michigan?" he asked. Maybe we could take a color tour."

After discussing the options, we decided to visit Michigan's

Upper Peninsula. Neither one of us had ever been there before. He said he'd look into flights to Grand Rapids or Detroit and rent a car and pick me up. He had to okay the trip with his probation officer.

"I don't think it'll be a problem," he said. "He's understanding, and I've been good."

The thought of spending a few days with Cooper made my heart sing. I missed him. Phone calls were good, but not a satisfying substitute for physical contact. "You made my day. I love you," I said.

The last few hours had been a roller coaster of emotions and events. Thankfully, it was ending on a high. But Grams' disapproval bothered me. I couldn't go to bed with her words ringing in my ears. I went downstairs where she was watching TV.

"Grams?" Using the remote, she turned down the volume but didn't say anything. "I'm sorry," I said. "What I did was wrong. Please, don't be mad at me."

She got up, came to me and held out her arms. We hugged. "I'm not mad, just scared. I don't want anything to happen to you. I know those hunts are wrong, but you could have been caught. Even worse, you could have been shot."

Being shot had never occurred to me. "I'm sorry to make you worry. It won't happen again." I told her Cooper might be coming and that we were thinking of going to the U.P.

"That's good. It'll be nice to see him again," she said.

"Yes, it will." I agreed.

"You're not going to tell him what you did, are you?" she asked. "The fewer people who know, the better."

"You don't think I can trust him? If I can't trust Cooper, I can't trust anybody." In my heart, I knew I would tell him, but only when the time was right. I couldn't keep such a secret from him.

"Okay, but nobody else. Promise?"

"Promise."

Grams turned the TV volume back up, and I went back up to bed.

Chapter 22

The shelter was closed on Sundays, but the animals still needed care. Today was my turn to go in and take care of things. I didn't mind. Sundays were all about the cats and dogs. If the phone rang, it was ignored. Voice mail could handle calls.

Working alone at the shelter was nothing new, but on this day I found myself jumpy. I double checked both doors that led outside to ensure they were locked. I also walked through the entire building just to make sure everything was in place and that I was alone. I had never felt the need to do that before.

"You're being ridiculous," I said out loud to myself. "Paranoid, is more like it," I answered.

I turned the radio on for company and started with the dogs. First step in the Sunday routine was food and water. Then I moved to the cat room. By the time I finished the cats, the dogs would be ready to go outside to do their business, and I could clean their kennels.

In the cat room, I scooped out litter boxes, poured kibble into bowls, provided fresh water and distributed catnip toys. Cages were about three feet off the floor so minimum bending was required. Each cage had two rooms separated by a wall with a round passageway. One area contained an elevated perch, a bed and bowls for food and water. The litter box was kept in the other space.

"Hey, Pumpkin, how you doing?" I said to an orange cat as he rubbed his head on my hand. He was more interested in being petted than food, so I obliged.

If beds were dirty, they were replaced. Any laundry generated on the weekends waited until Monday for the volunteers. The basics could be done in 30 minutes, but every cat begged for attention. Paws reached outside the cages trying to snag me when I got close. The talkers meowed asking to be noticed, and they couldn't be ignored. The half-hour job usually stretched to more than an hour, depending on how many cats were in residence. Today there were a dozen.

If they wanted, the cats could leave their cage while I cleaned. They would explore the room, sniffing and looking for mischief. Easygoing cats could stay out if they got along with others. When hissing and spitting started, someone had to be confined to a cage.

"Toby, are you coming out?" I asked a young black kitty. He jumped to the floor. "You know the routine." Toby had been a resident for more than two months––black cats usually took longer to get adopted. Most people preferred a more exotic look, like a calico, Siamese or tabby. "We'll find you a home, don't you worry," I told him.

Sometimes I'd take a seat so the lap cats could jump on me and get snuggle time. Like I said, the 30-minute job could easily double or triple in time. I didn't mind. I loved every minute. Getting to know the cats made it easier to answer questions when people came in to adopt. Some people wanted lap cats. Some didn't. Some wanted talkers. Some disliked vocal cats. Some wanted a cat colored just like the one they had had as a child.

The cats I trusted to behave were allowed to stay out while I took care of the dogs. Of course, the cats' wanderings were limited to the cat room.

"You guys be good. I'll be back," I told them.

The routine for the dogs was similar to that of the cats. We had two small outside dog runs where the dogs could play while their kennels were cleaned. I also liked to take the dogs for a walk for a lesson on how to walk on a leash. Basic training made them more adoptable.

For unknown reasons, I felt vulnerable when outside. Instead of focusing on the dogs, I kept watching the parking lot and road. The shooting and subsequent hiding at home under police protection apparently had consequences. I was jittery and anxious. Being alone had never bothered me before, but today it did.

"Get a grip," I told myself. I had to force myself to walk every dog.

By noon, I finished and happily locked up and left.

Back at home, Grams was cooking another batch of harvest stew. "This will definitely be the end of it," she said. "The garden is done for another year."

"Sad to see another summer end," I said. Normal conversation was appreciated.

"It'll be ready in an hour," she said.

There was an email from Cooper. He had booked a flight into Chicago for Tuesday. He'd rent a car and be here early evening. I hoped I could get time off work. I called Cindi at home and asked for a favor.

"Grams thinks I need a break, and I agree. This week has been too much. Is it okay if I take some time off?" After how I felt that morning at the shelter, I wasn't lying. A change of scenery would do me good, especially if the scenery included Cooper.

Cindi understood, but she was concerned about the workload at the shelter.

"I can come in Monday and line up volunteers to take care of the animals while I'm gone. I'll ask Carol to help with adoptions," I said. She asked if I was going somewhere or staying home. "I'm thinking of going on a road trip. A friend is coming to visit."

After dinner, I decided to take Dappy for a ride. It had been a while since I had last ridden. The feeling of vulnerability disappeared when I sat atop Dappy. We could outrun any danger.

We did the usual short ride—down the lane to the river, a short buzz by the water before cutting back to the lane and home again. Most of the trees had tinges of red and orange. A formation of geese honked overhead on their migration south.

"Before you know it, it's going to be snowing," I said to Dappy. His ears perked backwards listening to me.

Back at the barn, I took Buster for a walk around the yard. "You're going home soon," I told him. I hoped I was doing the right thing by him.

Everything seemed normal. The horses crunched on carrots. Bessie's calf was out of sight, but Bessie could be seen in the trees. Barn cats soaked up the afternoon sun, and the dogs lounged in the fenced-in portion of the yard.

Still, I couldn't shake the feeling that something was amiss.

Chapter 23

Seeing Cindi's car in the shelter's parking lot on Monday morning helped ease the tension I felt on the drive into work. Her car meant that I wouldn't be alone. While that felt good, I wondered how long my anxiety would last. I used to enjoy solitude. Now I feared being alone.

Cindi had coffee made and had brought in a box of assorted donuts.

"Thought we deserved a treat," she said as she poured us each a cup.

Instead of retreating back to her office with her coffee and donut, Cindi took a seat at the breakroom table. I accepted the unspoken invitation and sat down, too.

"Hard to say no to a donut," I said as I picked up an apple fritter. She asked if I had ever met Meg's husband. I hadn't. "Did you?"

"No. She never talked about him. I saw online there's a visitation Tuesday at Oak Grove. The funerals are Wednesday."

"Both of them?"

"The visitations are at the same time at the same place. The funerals are at different times."

"That makes it convenient," I said. "I'll miss the funerals, but I can make the visitations."

"Both obituaries asked that, instead of flowers, donations be made to the shelter. How generous is that?" Cindi said. "We'll have to do something special in their memory with the money."

That started a discussion of all the things the shelter could use: additional outside runs for dogs, a room where cats could be free-roaming instead of caged, a special fund for emergency veterinarian care, a fund for spay/neuter surgeries. "We'll have to see how many donations come in," Cindi said.

She questioned me about my plans. I asked if she recalled the handyman who once worked for Grams. "His name is Cooper," I reminded her. "Anyway, we've kept in touch with him, and he's coming to visit. His mother was a friend of Grams."

"You sweet on him?" she asked as she took a sip of coffee.

I hadn't told her about our relationship, but evidently it was obvious. I nodded my head up and down. "I am," I said.

She laughed. "If I remember right, you hated him when you first moved here."

"You remember right, but ... then I got to know him. He's a decent guy."

"When's he coming?"

"Tomorrow night. We plan on going to the U.P. Tuesday morning. That's why I'll miss the funerals."

Carol came in and joined us. I told her I was taking a few days off and asked if she could help cover for my absence.

"Are the donuts a bribe?" she asked.

"If they convince you to say yes, they are," I said as I picked up the box and held it out to her.

"They're a bonus," she said, selecting a long john. "I would have said yes without them."

She asked where I was going. I told her the truth: that the last few days had gotten the better of me and I needed a break, and that I was going on a color tour up north for a few days.

"I'll be back to work next Monday. I could come in tomorrow morning, too, if you need me."

She assured me she could handle things. Cindi and I both thanked her for all the work she did as a volunteer.

Carol admitted there was a reason she volunteered. "If there's ever money in the budget for part-time help, I hope you hire me," she said.

"Maybe next year," Cindi said. "I'll see if I can work it into the budget. I'd love to have the extra help, and you deserve to be paid. You do so much for us."

Carol and I worked together to clean and take care of the animals. The workload on Mondays was always double since we skimped on cleaning over the weekend. It was even worse this week since Jason had only done the bare essentials for two days.

A pile of dirty towels, blankets and cat beds greeted us in the laundry room. A stack of dirty water and food bowls sat on the counter next to the sink.

"Let's at least start a load of laundry before starting in the kennel," Carol said.

The sugar and caffeine gave us a jump start, and we buzzed nonstop through the work. By early afternoon, the cabinets were again stocked with clean bedding and bowls. The dogs had all been walked and were taking their afternoon siestas. The cats were resting with fresh catnip toys.

The afternoon was devoted to office work. Jason appeared as I was getting ready to leave for the day. I invited him into my office and told him I was taking a few days of vacation time.

"Any news on Meg's ex-husband?" I asked as he sat down.

"I heard he confessed. Meg filed for divorce, and he didn't want a divorce," he said.

I shared with him the times of the visitations and funerals. "It's going to be hard," I said. "I still can't believe they're both gone." I told him about the voice mail from Stanley's neighbor. "If he had called earlier, we would have known Stanley was up north. Would have saved us some grief," I said.

Jason shook his head in disbelieve. "That's a shame."

"I called the neighbor back and told him to tell Stanley that I'd bring his dog back in a couple weeks, that we wanted to make sure he was healed," I said. "I also told him to tell Stanley that there'd be no charge."

"Why the change of heart?"

"Everyone I talked to thought I was wrong. That if he was a good pet owner we should just give him the dog back and that it wasn't his fault the dog got caught in a trap."

"I think it's the right thing," he said. "When's he coming back?"

"I don't know."

I wondered if Stanley was hunting in the U.P. For a moment I wondered if going on a color tour during hunting season was a smart idea.

Jason stood up. He wished me a good vacation. "Don't do anything I wouldn't do," he said.

We both laughed.

"That's going to limit my fun," I said. "I'll call if I'm ever in doubt about what you would do."

After he left, I wondered why he had said what he did.

Chapter 24

Tuesday morning I spent packing and doing as many chores around the farm as I could to make things easier for Grams while I was gone. I made a run to the store for cat and dog food, plus kitty litter. I picked up poop in the yard and cleaned the litter boxes.

My habit of bringing home rescued animals increased the daily workload. Counting Buster, we were up to seven dogs. Five were mine. A few cats hitched a ride home with me, too. Ebony was the only one invited into the house; the rest were semi-feral and happy to be barn cats.

Fortunately, Grams used to board dogs for extra income, so she was used to having a full house. The fenced-in yard made it easier.

"What else can I do before I go?" I asked her.

"You've done enough. I'm old but not that old. I can handle things alone for a few days," she insisted.

After lunch, we changed clothes and left for the funeral home. At first, I thought it odd that both visitations were at the same time and same place but, once we arrived, it made sense. The caskets were in rooms across the hall from each other. Several people knew both women.

"It makes it easy for us," I said to Grams when we arrived.

We went to Dr. Katie's first. I didn't know any of her family, which made it awkward. We signed the guestbook. Looking around the crowded room, I didn't recognize anyone. "I don't even know if she was married or had children," I whispered to Grams.

"She was married. I'm pretty sure she has two or three kids. Grown. I bet some of those kids are her grandkids," she whispered, nodding to a group of youngsters sitting on a couch.

Poster boards covered with photographs rested on tripods on one side of the room. There were old photos of her as a child. Wedding pictures. Baby pictures. Vacation photos.

"So much I didn't know about her," I said.

A man in a black suit stood next to the casket talking to everyone who came up.

"I'm Alison, from the animal shelter," I said reaching out my hand. "I'm so sorry for your loss."

His name was Bob, and he was Katie's husband. "She told me about you," he said.

"She did a lot for us. We're going to miss her. I still can't believe this happened."

He gave me a hug. "I know," he said. "I don't know what I'm going to do without her."

I thanked him for asking that donations be given to the shelter. He nodded. Then I introduced him to Grams. They exchanged words of sympathy. We moved on, leaving him to greet the next guest.

We made our way out of the room and then went to see Meg. After signing the guest book, we looked at her photos. The poster boards had fewer photographs. Sad she wouldn't have children or grandchildren. I noticed none of her wedding pictures were included. Most photographs had her with a cat or a dog.

This time an older couple stood vigil by the casket.

"Must be her parents," I whispered to Grams.

Grams nodded and said she would wait for me.

When they were free, I walked up to them. "I'm so sorry," was all I could say. "So very sorry. You must be Meg's parents."

They both nodded yes. "How did you know Megan?" the woman asked.

"I work at the animal shelter. Dr. Katie did all our vet work. I got to know Meg when I'd take animals there," I told them.

"She loved animals. Ever since she was little she loved cats and dogs," the man said.

"And mice. And chickens. She loved them all," the woman said dabbing a tissue to her eyes.

"Thank you for suggesting donations be made to the shelter," I said.

"It's what she would have wanted," the mother said.

"We appreciate it." I gave each one a quick hug. "We'll let you know what we do with the money. I'm hoping it can be a lasting memorial."

"That would mean so much," Meg's dad said as he wiped his eyes with a tissue.

I didn't recognize anyone at Meg's visitation, so there was no one else to visit. After my brief talk with her parents, we left.

"So sad. I can't say I'm sorry I'm going to miss the funerals," I said on the way home.

Grams said she didn't plan on attending either.

My phone rang. It was Cooper. He had just gotten his rental car and would be leaving shortly. Our plan was to spend the night at the farm and leave in the morning. I couldn't wait to see him.

Back at the farm, we let the dogs out. Buddy got along so well with the other dogs that we no longer worried about the newcomer.

"He's part of the pack," Grams said.

It felt odd having the day off work. Since we only ate a light lunch, we were both hungry and decided to have an early dinner. Together we cooked a pot of spicy rice and beans. We spread the hot mixture on warm tortillas and added chopped lettuce, onion and tomato and rolled them up.

"I think we need to open a bottle of sweet red," I said. "How about that bottle of cherry wine from Leelanau Cellars?" We liked Michigan wines. This bottle was from a winery in Leelanau County near Traverse City just north of us.

Grams agreed. We carried our food, plates and the bottle of wine with two glasses out to the picnic table. "We won't be eating out here much longer," Grams said.

She was right. Already the heat of the summer had faded into cooler nights. "I'm not ready for winter," I said as I poured our drinks.

Grams held up her glass. "To Cooper," she said. I laughed, and we clinked glasses.

"To Cooper. May he soon be off probation and move here permanently," I said. The wine tasted sweet and zingy. "I like the wine," I added.

"Is that your plan?" Grams asked.

"It's my plan. The last we talked he agreed. I hope he hasn't changed his mind." I spread a napkin on my lap and placed a rolled tortilla on each of our plates. I didn't tell her about all my plans. The plan of starting a family. A baby. I needed to make sure Cooper agreed before I shared that news.

Grams took a sip of her wine as I served the food. "It *is* good. We'll have to remember this one and get more."

Drinking wine on an empty stomach left me feeling light and smiley. The tortillas tasted delicious. As we ate, I took a moment to appreciate life. The dogs played in the fenced-in yard, the sun warmed my back, the food was tasty and the wine sweet. I couldn't ask for a better place to live, and Grams was the best roommate. Life was perfect, and I was excited about the future.

I filled our glasses again and lifted mine for another toast. "To us. May we always be this blessed."

Grams lifted her glass to meet mine. "To us," she said.

Chapter 25

Feeling fine from the wine didn't keep us from doing the evening chores. As I walked Buster around the yard, Grams gave grain to the horses and fed the barn cats.

"Bessie," Grams shouted toward the pasture. We waited, but Bessie ignored the invitation to dinner. "I think it's time to have a talk with that cow."

Without alcohol pulsating through our veins, I doubt if we'd have climbed the fence and gone out to confront the protective mother, but that's exactly what we did, with Buster in tow. Grams carried a bucket of grain and carrots.

"Let's talk as we walk like nothing special is happening," Grams said as we made our way toward the grove of trees where we knew Bessie was hiding her little one.

"Well, that should be easy," I replied, but my mind went blank on what to say.

"Don't show any fear," Grams advised.

"I wasn't feeling any fear until you brought it up. Now I'm a little worried. Why should we be scared?"

"Mothers are unpredictable. Bessie's protecting her calf. Just keep an eye on her and be ready to move."

"Maybe I shouldn't have brought Buster."

"No, I think he'll have a calming effect on her."

Bessie came into view with her babe behind her. When we got closer, Grams called her name. "We're bringing dinner," she added.

Grams held out the pail, hoping the aroma of the sweet feed and carrots would entice Bessie, but she didn't move forward, so we kept walking.

"At least she's not running away," I said, recalling the days I spent trying to catch her when she escaped from the overturned truck. Back then, she had a knack of staying just out of reach, but now she stood her ground and watched as we approached.

"We're not here to take your baby," Grams softly said. "We just want to meet him ... or her. I promise you can keep your calf."

We were able to walk right up to Bessie. Grams set the bucket down in front of her and patted her neck as she lowered her head to eat. I reached out and rubbed her back. The calf tucked his head under her belly and started sucking. Buster walked over and sniffed the baby's feet.

"Now what?" I asked, continuing to rub Bessie's neck.

Grams walked around to the side of her. "Good girl," she said. Keeping one hand on Bessie, she was able to touch the calf. Bessie lifted her head and turned it toward Grams. I held my breath, but nothing happened. Bessie kept chewing. She turned back and continued to eat.

"Well, that was easy," I said.

Grams petted the calf. "It's a boy," she said. "What shall we name him?"

"Lucky? No, that's too boring. What do you think?"

"Let's get to know him. Something will come to us."

After Bessie licked the bucket clean, we carried it back to the barn, leaving Bessie alone with her calf.

"I think she's starting to realize she's safe here," Grams said.

I kept Buster with us as we returned to the picnic table. Grams filled our wine glasses again, which finished off the bottle. The sun slipped lower into the west.

"Cooper should be here soon," Grams said.

As she spoke, I noticed headlights coming down the road. "Maybe that's him," I said, pointing in the direction of the oncoming vehicle.

We watched a black Jeep Wrangler pull into the driveway. It was him.

Grams and I both greeted Cooper with hugs when he got out of the Jeep. Grams asked if he was hungry. He nodded yes. She scurried to the kitchen, leaving us alone. I introduced him to Buster. He squatted and petted the dog with both hands.

"Hey, boy, how ya doing? Too bad about the leg, but you'll be fine." Buster's wagging tail told me he approved of this stranger.

Cooper looked good with his California tan, tight fitting jeans and tucked-in shirt.

"Nice wheels. I was expecting a car," I said.

"I thought this would be more fun. I read that the U.P. has some rough roads and a four-wheel drive is a good idea."

"Sounds fun," I said. "How was the drive?"

"Stop and go in Chicago. As I got away from the city, it got better and better."

"Your hair's getting long again," I said, reaching out and running my fingers through his golden locks. The last time I saw him he had a prison buzz-cut. I preferred the blond curls that came with the shaggy look.

"Just needed a change. You're looking good," he said, grabbing me and giving me a kiss.

Being together after not seeing each other for months was awkward. Phone calls were good, but it almost felt like I was in a relationship with two different people––the man I talked to on the phone every night, and this one. With the phone guy, I didn't concern myself with what I wore or my body language or how my hair looked. Those things seemed to matter with the in-person boyfriend.

"Thanks. We're having a fun evening. Eating, drinking and hanging out with the critters."

"Sounds perfect to me."

Grams came out with a plate of rolled tortillas and another bottle of cherry wine. She also had a battery-operated lantern. She led us from the car to the picnic table. I excused myself to put Buster back in the barn.

"I'm starved. I didn't have much for lunch," I heard Cooper tell Grams as I walked to the barn.

"You're a good boy," I told Buster as I gave him a treat.

As I left the barn, I took a moment to breathe and appreciate the scene before me. The sky blazed with red as the sun settled into the west. Grams had turned on the little lantern. In the glow of the light, I watched Cooper eat and Grams sip on her wine. Life was good.

"Here," Grams said as I approached the table. She held my glass out to me. She had filled it again. I took it and held it up.

"Here's to a perfect Michigan evening," I said. "Good food, good friends and life."

Grams and Cooper both held up their glasses.

"This is good ... for a Michigan wine," Cooper said after he took a sip.

Grams lightly slapped his arm. "Don't be silly," she said.

He laughed, a soft throaty laugh accompanied by a smile that took over his whole face.

I loved hearing him laugh.

"All right, let me reword that," he said. "It's good. The perfect choice for a Michigan night."

Twilight settled around us as we talked. We told Cooper about our encounter with Bessie's calf and how she finally allowed us to meet her baby.

"Maybe you can meet them in the morning before we leave," I said.

Cooper filled us in on his parents and his grandmother.

When we drained the last wine from the bottle, we called it a night and headed into the house. The dogs were excited to see Cooper, and he gave each one attention. Like with Buster, Cooper squatted and petted Buddy with both hands.

"He's doing better than I expected," I said.

"It's obvious that Rocky and his group know what they're doing," he said.

"They do. They've been doing it for years."

Grams settled in to watch TV. Cooper and I went upstairs. I wanted to tell him about my picture in the paper and how I had set the whitetail deer free, but I didn't want to ruin the mood, and the mood was good. The wine fueled our passion. All was right in my world as I fell asleep in Cooper's arms.

Chapter 26

Keeping a secret from Cooper haunted me. It felt like a thunderstorm hovering over my head that could, at any time, let loose and have serious consequences. To tell or not to tell, I didn't want to spend the next week ruminating.

The three-hour time difference between California and Michigan left Cooper exhausted. He snored and I lay awake. I could hear the breathing of the dogs as they slept on their beds. I decided to tell him before we got up. I thought of possible opening lines:

I have something to tell you.

I need to tell you something before we get up.

Promise me you won't be mad.

Did you know there are hunting preserves really close to here?

Before we get up, I need to get something off my chest.

I haven't been truthful, and I have to share something with you.

Don't say anything until I'm done talking.

I'm not sure what time I drifted off to sleep, but when I woke, the resolution to tell was still strong. In the end, all of the opening lines I had thought of made it into my confession.

"Are you awake?" I asked when Cooper moved.

"Almost," he answered.

"Do you remember when you told me that I was almost in the Save Five Club? That all I needed to do was save an animal from hunting?" I asked.

"That's how you say good morning?" he asked. He wore a smile as he reached over to give me a kiss.

"I've got something I need to tell you. Can you just listen?" I sat cross-legged and looked down at him. I wanted to see his face.

"I'm listening," he said resting on his back.

I told him about the hunting preserves for whitetail deer and the deceptive name of Whitey's Whitetail Sanctuary. At the end of my description, I told him I was a member of the Save Five Club.

"What?" He sat up and stared at me. "What did you do?" he asked in a terse, controlled voice.

"Cut the fence and peeled it back so the deer could escape. Twice. At two different places. But one had cameras. I didn't know that, so my picture was in the newspaper. But I was wearing a disguise. The one I wore to the dog fight. It's a blurry black and white picture. I really look like a guy."

"Nobody recognized you?"

"Only Grams. They're offering a reward to anyone with information. Grams wants me to lay low for a few days. Hence the vacation. So that makes me a member of the club, right? The newspaper said several deer escaped."

I thought he would be proud of me, but he didn't say anything. A sober stare replaced the playful smile.

"I'm done. That's my story," I said trying to add a little levity to the situation.

He still didn't say anything.

"I didn't want to tell you over the phone," I explained wanting to fill the silence. "Say something."

"Prison isn't fun. Yes, I want you to fight for animals, but I want you to do it legally. I thought you would have learned from my mistake. I don't want to see you going to prison. It would kill me. I don't want anything to happen to you," he said with a low, serious voice.

"You're right. I wasn't thinking. I just got so mad when I read their websites. The deer don't have a chance. They're guaranteed hunts. I don't understand who would find that sport, but apparently a lot of people do," I said. "I promise I won't do it again. Forgive me?"

It took him a few seconds to answer. When he did, I wasn't so sure I believed him, but the words were right.

"Of course, I forgive you. No secrets. I'm glad you told me."

Blue jumped on the bed. Shadow and Cody stood by the door. Their way of telling me they wanted to go out. Buddy sat on the floor watching.

"We'd better get going," I said.

Cooper answered by swinging his legs to the floor and sitting on the side of the bed,

I put on a robe. "Let's go guys," I said. I escorted the dogs downstairs and let them out. Grams sat at the kitchen table drinking coffee.

"Can I make breakfast for you guys before you leave?" she asked.

"Sure, but we need to shower. It'll be a few minutes before we're ready."

Back upstairs, the bed was empty, and I could hear the shower running. Cooper stuck his head out the door. "Join me?"

Instead of shouting, yes, I smiled and accepted his invitation by taking off my robe and pulling my nightgown over my head.

After a hearty breakfast of vegan blueberry pancakes, we went to the barn. The morning had an autumn chill, but the blue sky promised a warm day.

"Look," I said pointing. "Bessie brought her calf up."

"How cute is that?" Cooper said. "He's a mini Bessie. He looks just like her."

The horses ignored the little guy. I imagined that Dappy, Chester and MaryLu had already snuck out to Bessie's hiding spot and congratulated her on the baby.

"Bessie's smart. She's realizing we can be trusted," Grams said as she slipped between the wooden boards of the fence and walked up to the new mom while the calf nursed.

"You have a sweet little fella," Grams said, patting Bessie with one hand and the baby with the other.

"Hey, what about Fella for his name?" I said.

"Fella," Grams said, sounding it out. "I don't know. It's in the running, but let's keep thinking," she suggested as she rubbed her hand over the calf's back and down his rear legs. His tail swatted back and forth.

"You're going to get to keep that tail," she told him.

Bessie's tail had been docked. Docking was a dairy industry tradition to keep the tail from flinging crud into the farmer's face as he hooked up the milking machine. Without a tail, Bessie couldn't swish flies off herself.

"There's no end to the way people torture animals," Cooper said as he rubbed my back. "I understand why you did what you did."

Grams quit playing with the calf and turned to me. "You told him?" She sounded angry.

"I did. I can't keep secrets from him."

"I'm glad she told me," Cooper said. "And I asked her not to do it again. Not to do anything illegal."

"Listen to him," Grams ordered.

I held up my right hand as if taking an oath. "I promise both of you. No more breaking the law."

We took Buster for a walk and fed the barn cats. Then we started loading the Jeep.

"I almost forgot. We need to bring towels and sheets for one of the places we're staying at," Cooper said.

"Really? What kind of place makes you bring your own bedding?"

"It's a cabin at a campground. With a view of the Bridge. Something different from a hotel," Cooper explained. "We have to stay two nights. I booked it for Friday and Saturday.

In my room, I stuffed pillows, sheets, a blanket and towels into jumbo size garage bags, and Cooped lugged them to the Jeep.

"I think that's it," I said as I surveyed the contents in the cargo space.

We hugged Grams goodbye. I felt a twinge of guilt leaving her, but it passed when she gave me a kiss and whispered, "I love you. Have fun and don't worry about me."

Chapter 27

The Jeep still had a new-car smell. As I settled into the passenger seat, Cooper handed me a Michigan map and an atlas filled with county maps.

"Really? Why not use the GPS?"

"There're places up north where it won't work so we need maps," he said. "I have the first part of the trip mapped out. We're taking U.S. 31 to the Mackinac Bridge. It's less than 200 miles. Should take us about four hours."

"You did your homework."

"I have reservations for us tonight in Sault Ste. Marie at the Lockview Motel," he said. "It's right by the Soo Locks so we can watch the ships go through the locks."

"Sounds interesting," I said. Actually, the thought of watching ships sounded boring, but I had never watched locks operate, so maybe it would be more exciting than I anticipated.

I unfolded the map and found Scottville and U.S. 31 and glanced at the route Cooper had selected. We'd be going through Traverse City, Charlevoix and Petoskey. I'd never been farther north than Traverse City. I'd never crossed the Mackinac Bridge either–– it connected Mackinaw City to St. Ignace in the Upper Peninsula. I Googled the bridge and found it had its own website.

I read to Cooper as he drove. "'It's the longest suspension bridge in the Americas, with a total length of 8,614 feet suspended. It is currently the third longest suspension bridge in the world.'

"'Much of the beauty comes from the setting at the Straits of Mackinac. The Straits link Lake Michigan and Lake Huron. The five-mile-long Mackinac Bridge (Big Mac) links Michigan's Lower and Upper Peninsulas.'

"'Ground was broken to build the Mackinac Bridge on May 7, 1954, and the bridge opened to the public (and the ferries were shut down) on November 1, 1957.'

"Is it longer than the Golden Gate?" I asked. Cooper lived near San Francisco, and when I visited him, we drove over the iconic bridge.

"The Big Mac bridge itself is longer, but the Golden Gate's span between towers is longer," Cooper explained.

"Get this, two people died when their vehicles went over the edge. One was a Yugo and the other a Ford Bronco. If you're too scared to drive across the bridge, they have people who will drive your car across," I said, starting to get nervous about the crossing.

"Only two in 50-some years isn't bad," Cooper said.

"Unless you're one of the two," I said as I continued to read. "Here's good news, they close the bridge when it gets too windy."

"Let's hope that doesn't happen."

After our lesson about the bridge, I put the phone and maps away and enjoyed the scenery of autumn's yellows, reds and oranges. The muted gray sky threatened rain, but it stayed dry.

U.S. 31 was a two-lane paved road that curved and zigzagged through small towns. Occasionally, we'd get close enough to the big lake to catch a glimpse of the water.

Time flew by. It didn't feel like four hours had passed, but it wasn't long before road signs announced the last chance to exit before the Mackinac Bridge.

"No wind. We won't be swimming today," Cooper teased.

Then we were on it. Green suspension cables and railings edged both sides of the bridge. The cables increased in length as they neared the top of the support tower. The bridge was four lanes with the center two lanes grated.

"You comfortable driving?" I asked.

"Doesn't bother me. I'm used to driving the Golden Gate." He stayed in the grated left lane, which rumbled as we drove on it.

The sun peeked out as we crossed, making the water below a crystal blue. It shimmered with the noonday light. Cooper pointed out a cargo ship in the distance.

We paid the toll as we left the bridge on the northern side. We stopped in St. Ignace for gas, and then continued on I-75 for

50 miles to Sault Ste. Marie. The landscape flattened out, but the fall colors still performed. The sun retreated again, and this time the threat of rain was no longer a warning. It started gently, but soon the wipers were on high speed to keep the road visible.

"I forgot my umbrella," I said.

"We won't need it," Cooper said. "If it rains, we'll stay inside. In bed."

"Well, let's hope for rain then," I said.

I put the motel's address into my phone, and the GPS worked fine getting us there. After we exited I-75, we made a couple turns, and then drove down a road lined with stores and restaurants.

When directed, we turned left onto Portage Avenue. The Lockview Motel was just a couple blocks down and directly across from the Soo Locks Park. Hanging baskets of pink petunias greeted us as we turned into the motel's narrow driveway. On each side of the drive was a row of doors and windows, each with limited parking in front. The mom-and-pop operation was to my liking.

After checking in and unloading our bags, we climbed back in the Jeep to go in search of a late lunch. We discovered that vegan food was scarce and ended up at a Subway eating veggie subs. We then went to a grocery store and bought lettuce, spinach, tomatoes and other fixings for a salad, plus hummus, guacamole and crackers. We also bought a bag of pistachios and a bottle of wine.

We stashed the food in our room and then walked to the park. The park, enclosed with a black wrought-iron fence, had a uniformed guard who asked questions and checked backpacks and purses before allowing people inside. He asked where we were from, and our answers satisfied him. We didn't have any bags for him to search.

First stop was the visitor's center where there were countless displays and tidbits of information about the locks. The locks were on the St. Mary's River, which connected Lake Superior to Lake Huron. They also had a monitor that showed when freighters were expected.

"One should be here in 20 minutes," Cooper said. "Let's go."

A two-story observation platform stood a short distance away. The top deck provided the best view of the four parallel locks.

To the west, the yellowish-beige, International Bridge connected Michigan to Canada.

Cooper struck up a conservation with a guy on the platform. Cooper had questions, and the young man, who apparently made freighters a hobby, had answers. Cooper devoured the facts. I just listened.

Only one lock was big enough to handle the big ships. Most carried bulk cargo, such as limestone, iron ore, grain, coal or salt from the mines and farms of the upper Great Lakes. They transported the materials south to industrial areas around the lakes.

"There's a 21-foot difference in elevation between Lake Superior and Lake Huron," the guy told Cooper. "There used to be rapids along here that stopped ships from going through. The locks work by gravity, not pumps. After a boat comes in from Lake Superior, the gates at each end of the locks are closed. A valve is opened to let the Lake Superior water flow out to the lower water level of the St Mary's and Lake Huron."

We watched as a mammoth freighter approached from Lake Superior and slowly inched into the lock. Once in, a handful of men tied up the ship. Then the huge gates closed. The freighter rested within inches of the side of the lock. Gradually, the ship started to go down as the water level dropped. It took about 20 minutes. Then the gates at the other end opened, and the ship started its slow march to the lower great lake.

It reminded me of Gordon Lightfoot's song "The Wreck of the Edmund Fitzgerald," and I wondered how many times the Edmund Fitzgerald passed through these locks.

"Look, another one is coming," Cooper said, pointing to a ship in the east.

"Does that mean you want to stay?"

"Don't you?" He seemed surprised by my question. Surprised I wasn't fascinated or impressed with seeing freighters up close.

"Just asking. If you want to stay, we can."

So we stayed and watched the whole operation in reverse. This time the ship went up as gravity filled the locks with Lake Superior water. When the water level in the locks equaled that of the western St. Mary's River, the gates opened and the freighter continued its trip to Lake Superior.

After the second ship sailed into the sunset, we strolled around the park and enjoyed the flowerbeds, towering maple trees and water fountain. Our education wasn't done—there were historical markers, informative displays and ship models sprinkled throughout the park. Cooper read every word of every display.

Traveling is tiring. Back in the room, Cooper opened a bottle of wine. We fixed a salad and had some crackers and dips. Since we wanted to get an early start, we went to bed early.

Chapter 28

We walked to the Lockview Restaurant for breakfast. Meat and eggs dominated the menu. We ordered the usual vegan fare—oatmeal, hash browns, fruit and coffee. The place lived up to its name. Seated by the window, we could see the Soo Locks Visitor Center, observation platform and freighters as they passed through the locks.

We didn't need to pack, because we were returning for a second night at the old-fashion motel. Cooper had the day planned: Tahquamenon Falls and the Great Lakes Shipwreck Museum at Whitefish Point.

"That's where the Edmund Fitzgerald went down," I said. "Whitefish Bay." The only reason I knew that was from the Gordan Lightfoot song. The haunting song was now stuck on replay in my head. "Where are we going first?" I asked as we got in the Jeep.

"The lower Tahquamenon Falls. Then the upper falls. They're four miles apart. There's a hiking trail along the river, but we'll save that for another day," he said.

Again, the GPS on the phone worked, so we didn't have to worry about navigating. The falls were about 70 miles away.

An employee at the lower falls explained that there were a series of five smaller falls. The best view was from an island in the river. Row boats were available for rent.

"Do you know how to row?" I asked Cooper.

The woman at the counter overheard me and told us that no experience was needed. "It's not far. It'll take you less than five minutes. Just pull the boat up on shore and remember which one is yours," she said. "There's a half-mile hiking trail around the island."

Cooper pulled out his wallet and paid the rental fee. The woman helped me into the boat while Cooper settled into the rowing seat. He picked up the oars and we were off. We zigzagged until he got the feel of making the boat go where he wanted it to go. Then he rowed us in circles, just for the fun of it. As the water dripped from the oars, I noticed it was yellowish-brown in color.

"I expected the water up here to be clean," I said.

As usual, Cooper had done his homework and had an answer. "I read that the amber color is caused by the leaching of tannic acid from the cedar and hemlock swamps," he said. He pointed out the distant falls where the cascading water had a golden hue. Cooper maneuvered the boat to a dock where we were able to get out. Then we pulled the boat up onto shore. There were no other boats.

"Looks like we have the place to ourselves," I said.

"Perfect," Cooper replied.

The trail was a loop so we could go either way.

"Which way?" I asked.

The falls we saw while rowing were to the right, so that's the direction we headed. The trail was rugged. Tree roots and rocks were like speed bumps forcing us to go slow and appreciate the beauty. As we got closer, the roar of the tumbling river intensified. A curve in the path revealed a rock outcrop that offered a natural viewing platform. Boulders provided seating. Autumn's tapestry of yellow and orange perfected the breathtaking scene.

The morning air still had a tinge of chill. Lazily sitting on a rock and soaking up the sun made me feel like a turtle, but nothing could scare me enough to jump into the river. I watched as Cooper made his way closer to the falls while taking photographs with his phone. The sorrows and scares of the last week melted away. Grams was right—I needed this break. Cooper turned and pointed the phone in my direction. I smiled and waved. He came back and sat down on a boulder next to mine.

"I wanted a *before* picture," he said.

"Before what?"

He stood up and then knelt down on one knee in front of me. "Before I asked you to marry me. I love you and want us to spend the rest of our lives together. I love your tenacity, your independence, your kindness. Will you marry me?"

Stunned, shocked and almost speechless best described my reaction as Cooper held out a ring box. I didn't notice the ring. I focused on his face. His usual smile replaced with an intense seriousness.

"Yes," I said. "Hell, yes. I'd be honored to be your wife."

I slid off the rock, landing on my feet as Cooper stood up. His intensity evaporated and the smile returned. Our passion matched that of the water rushing over the rocky falls. This is why Cooper was pleased that we would be alone on the island.

Cooper placed the ring on my finger. The yellow gold band matched the amber river. The diamond sparkled like the sun-glittered water of the Great Lakes. The ring fit perfectly.

"How did you know my ring size?"

"Grams. I asked her. She had to ask your mother." I flashed back to the day spent with my mother sorting through stuff when she decided to downsize. She offered me her costume jewelry. Her style wasn't mine, so I didn't accept any of the flashy necklaces or bracelets. I had tried on rings, so she would have known my ring size.

"So, they both know?"

"Grams does. I'm guessing your mother does too," he said.

I laughed. Grams, with her philosophy of no secrets, had kept a secret.

"We need an *after* photo," Cooper said. We grinned together for a selfie with the river as a background, but my ring finger dominated the scene.

Hands clasped, we continued following the trail. The proposal eclipsed the rest of the walk, as autopilot took over, and I wrestled with my new normal. I was engaged.

Chapter 29

Before sightseeing at the upper falls, we lunched at the Tahquamenon Falls Brewery & Pub. "We're not going to like the décor, but they do have vegan options," Cooper said as we pulled into the parking lot. "It's an oddity. A restaurant pub on state land, but it used to be a logging camp. The owners' grandparents sold the land to the state with an agreement that it be maintained as a recreational area. They were smart enough to demand the right to have a business on the land. Besides the restaurant and pub, there's a gift store."

Cooper nailed it when he said we wouldn't like the decor. Dead animals dominated. A full-size, stuffed black bear greeted us at the door. On the walls were pelts stretched taut, reminding me of chalk outlines at crime scenes. The fur was beautiful, but I'm sure it was more handsome on its original owner. Marble eyes of bodiless deer, elk and moose stared at us as we took a seat. Birds, motionless in midflight, clung to the wall.

Wood tables and chairs, a huge stone fireplace and a cathedral ceiling of wooden beams completed the rustic feel.

Our options included pasta marinara, a veggie sandwich or a cherry-walnut salad with fresh bread. Nice to have choices. We started lunch with an appetizer of bruschetta without cheese and blueberry ale. Cooper ordered the pasta. I preferred the salad.

"Here's to us," Cooper toasted after the server brought the glasses of ale.

Despite being surrounded by death, I enjoyed lunch. My left-hand thumb kept reaching across my palm and feeling the slim band that encircled my finger next to the pinkie. The ring felt foreign and a little uncomfortable. Cooper's proposal still left me flabbergasted, but in a good way. Thinking of a life with him made me smile, made me happy.

After lunch, we stopped in the gift shop. It, too, was decorated with the skins, heads and fur of wildlife. We didn't stay long. Once outside, we followed signs to the path that would take us to the falls. Holding hands, we entered the woods, greeted by autumn's welcome-mat of fallen golden leaves. The trail, with various viewing platforms, followed the Tahquamenon River. Glimpses of the falls teased us. The river was wider and the drop higher than the previous falls.

"It's so much bigger," I remarked.

"If I remember right, the drop is close to 50 feet," Cooper explained.

An older couple sat on a bench at the top of the stairs leading to the main observation deck.

"It's 94 steps down," said the guy.

"And 94 steps back up," said the woman.

"Is it worth it?" I asked.

"Yes," they chorused together.

We all laughed.

"Did you know the locals call Tahquamenon Falls the Root Beer Falls?" the man asked.

"No, I didn't know that. Did you?" I asked Cooper.

"I didn't."

The wife didn't wait for us to guess about the nickname. "Because of the brown color of the water. When it crashes at the bottom, it creates a white frothy foam that looks like root beer."

"I didn't know that. I'll watch for it," I acknowledged.

We said goodbye to the couple and headed down the stairs.

"That's us in 50 years," I offered.

"I hope in 50 years we can still climb 94 steps," Cooper joked.

The thought of sharing 50 years with Cooper melted my heart. I grabbed his hand to make sure he was real.

The falls announced their presence with a thunderous roar that increased as we descended. The close-up view was worth the workout. With the 50-foot drop, the amber color was more evident than at the shorter falls. And sure enough, at the bottom, a brown, frothy foam bubbled. We joined the other tourists taking photographs and selfies. The vista was deserving of the attention. Leaning on the wooden railing, I stared in wonderment as the current rushed the water along. Then the riverbed vanished, and the unsuspecting water tumbled and roared. After creating a splash and the root-beer froth, it continued on its way to become one with Lake Superior.

Cooper jarred me back to reality with his time constraints. "The Shipwreck Museum is only open until six, so we need to get going."

"How far away is it?"

"Not far, about 20 minutes."

Checking the time on my phone, I noted that it was already past three, and we still had to hike back to the parking lot. So we hurried. No time for long goodbyes, just one last look at the majestic Tahquamenon Falls.

It was almost four when we pulled into the museum's parking lot. I expected to see one building, but the museum was a compound with a lighthouse and several buildings. Its location at Whitefish Point was at the extreme southeastern end of Lake Superior.

With limited time, I first wanted to see the exhibit of the Edmund Fitzgerald. It had more information than I could take in. Again, Gordon Lightfoot's song looped in my head.

The ship's display included the original bell that had been recovered from the sunken ship. The ship sank on November 10, 1975. Gale warnings had been issued, as winds gusted up to 50 knots and waves were 12 to 16 feet high. All 29 members of the crew died. My heart cried for the men and their families. Again, Cooper broke my trance.

"There's more to see. If we hurry we can tour the lighthouse tower." Grabbing my hand, he pulled me away to continue the self-guided tour.

"More stairs," I whined.

"Only 56," he replied.

My legs complained but obeyed. When I reached the top, I concluded that the climb had been worth it when I saw the panoramic view of the rooftops and distant waters of Whitefish

Bay and Lake Superior. Gentle waves lapped at the rocky beach. I couldn't imagine being on a freighter in waves so high that they somehow compromised the safety underfoot.

Cooper read aloud. "'Whitefish Point Light is the oldest operating lighthouse on Lake Superior. The present light tower was constructed in 1861 during Abraham Lincoln's administration.'"

"Really? That's hard to believe," I said.

We had run out of time but were able to stroll along the beach. A sign told us that it was illegal to take stones from the beach.

"Just one?" I begged Cooper.

"How soon you forgot your promise to stay above the law," he teased.

"I didn't mean for that promise to cover everything. Just animal stuff," I joked. In the end, I didn't steal any stones.

The day wore us out, and we still had an hour's drive back to Sault Ste. Marie.

"Do you want to look for a place for dinner or go back to the room and eat what we bought yesterday?" Cooper asked.

Knowing the odds were against finding something we wanted to eat, I voted for supper in our room. "A glass of wine sounds tasty," I said.

As we headed south, the sun began its descent in the west, creating a palette of purples and reds.

"It's the kind of sky that wouldn't look real in a painting," I noted. "I've never seen anything like it."

Cooper pulled over next to a small lake so we could take in the evening show. The colors reflected on the water and, as the sun continued its westward path, the beauty morphed but remained spectacular. When the performance ended, we stood silent outside the Jeep for a few moments, Cooper's arm draped around my shoulder.

"It's been a good day," I confessed.

Chapter 30

On Friday morning, Cooper suggested we go geocaching. He had introduced me to the game when we were searching for my beagle, Blue, the time he had been stolen from Grams' yard. We used geocaching as an excuse to trespass on an old farm where we thought we might find him.

"While you were in the shower I looked for interesting caches," Cooper informed me. "I found one with several good reviews. It's an old abandoned limestone quarry that's now owned by a conservation group."

"Where is it?"

"Somewhere between here and the bridge. We'll have to use the phone to get there."

"So much for the phone not working up here," I replied.

"Doesn't hurt to have backup."

We packed, checked out and had a last breakfast at the Lockview Restaurant. As we finished eating, Cooper spotted a freighter coming into the locks.

"Let's go see one more," he suggested.

So we did. From the top floor of the viewing deck, we watched as the red and white *CSL Laurentien* inched its way into the locks. The gates closed, the water slowly emptied and the ship dropped. As it moved into St. Mary's River, we left the park.

In the Jeep, Cooper handed me the phone for navigation. Looking at the phone, I said, "We go west on M-28, like we're heading back to the falls. Then we'll go south on M-123 to Trout Lake Road."

The drive was easy, but remote. Most of the way we traveled through the Hiawatha National Forest. We felt like we were home when we finally found Fiborn Quarry Road, but the adventure was just beginning.

We saw a small parking lot, but it was a distance from the cache. A gravel road continued to the left, which at least was in the right direction, so we took it. The road narrowed but remained passable.

"We're close," I said. The GPS and map on the geocaching app showed we were about a quarter mile away. We got out to walk, but it didn't take long to realize it was the wrong approach. A sign told us to keep back and beware of steep drop-offs. We had reached the side of the quarry. Apparently, the cache was hidden on the quarry floor, and we were on the ridge above it.

"Let's go back to the parking lot," Cooper advised. I agreed. Turning the Jeep around on the narrow road took several back-and-forth maneuvers.

"This looks better," Cooper commented when we neared a parking lot we had bypassed. A wooden sign welcomed us to the Fiborn Karst Preserve. It told us not to climb quarry walls, that there were unsafe buildings, fires were not permitted and only foot traffic was allowed.

The GPS pointed us in the direction of the cache. "It's a half mile away," I noted.

There were two options, both in the direction we wanted to go. We could follow a well-worn two-track along the woods or walk on the quarry floor. We opted for the second choice.

After only a couple minutes of walking, I felt transported to another planet. Underfoot was chiseled gray rock. Cracks in the inhospitable surface gave shrubs and saplings opportunity to take root. Nature was healing the scars from mining. The ground was littered with small jagged rocks that we guessed were limestone. The barren landscape felt desolate, and I had a sense of trespassing, even though I knew we weren't.

"This place has a weird vibe," I whispered. Using my normal voice seemed out of place.

"It does. Not sure why," Cooper replied softly.

There were also several small ponds of water.

"Wow, look at that," I exclaimed. In front of us loomed remnants of concrete buildings. Most of their wood had long since rotted away. As we got closer, we noticed a sign: "Historic Buildings, 1905. Please treat with respect.

We walked through a doorway—its wooden door long gone—into a cavernous room with several large windows with the glass missing. A feeling of reverence enveloped me. It was like walking in a cemetery. In several places, black-stick dancing figures had been painted on the walls. One fellow with a white bowtie boogied with a broom, couples twirled and kicked up their feet and one guy stood holding a suitcase next to train tracks. *Were they once workers or residents of this ghost town?*

"I wonder when these were painted?" I remarked. We couldn't tell if the primitive graffiti was recent or decades old. Either way, the drawings added fuel to my uneasy feeling.

After leaving the building, we focused on finding the cache, which wasn't hard to find. It was a military ammo box hidden in a pile of rocks. We signed the log book and replaced it as we had found it.

We walked through another relic structure that we thought might have been used for loading limestone into railcars. Each end of this building had an opening big enough for a train to go through. A hole in the ceiling looked suitable for dropping rocks into a rail car. From there we followed the railroad bed, the tracks long gone. It turned out to be the trail we didn't take from the parking lot.

"I want a souvenir chunk of limestone," I said. "The sign didn't say anything about not taking limestone."

Cooper helped me load a big piece of limestone into the back of the Jeep. As we drove away, my feeling of security returned.

Since the day was young, Cooper decided to go sightseeing on the backroads. Just when our faith in modern technology had been restored by the phone successfully leading us to the Fiborn cache, we lost the GPS signal. After driving around, we also lost our sense of direction. There weren't any houses, only forests. When we came to an intersection, we could only guess which way to go.

"We could flip a coin," I suggested. "Tails for left, heads for right." We followed the quarter's lead and went right.

"Can't go wrong with right," I joked.

After driving a couple miles, we saw a pickup truck parked on the side of the road. Two guys stood off to one side.

"I wonder if they need help," I said. The truck was pointed in the direction from which we had just come.

"Maybe they can give us directions," Cooper commented as he pulled off the road.

As I watched, Cooper walked over to talk to the men. I noted that the truck looked familiar. Where had I seen a black, beat up pickup? Then it hit me. It was Stanley Jones' truck. I recalled Stanley's neighbor saying he was in the U.P. What are the odds we'd run into him? I got out of the Jeep with the intention of talking to Stanley about his dog. Then I noticed a dead deer in the back of the truck. Disgusted, I turned around and got back into the Jeep. When Cooper returned, he said the guys were able to give him directions back to M-123.

"That was Stanley Jones," I told him.

"Who?"

"Let's go," I said, wanting to put distance between me and Stanley. After Cooper pulled away, I continued. "He's the guy who owns Buster. I recognized his truck. I was going to go talk to him, but then I saw the deer." Cooper's back had been turned so he didn't see me exit the Jeep and then turn right around and get back in, but I was sure Stanley had seen me. Did he recognize me?

"Did he say anything about me?" I asked Cooper.

"No, he just said they didn't need help. I told him we were lost and he gave me directions."

"He's poaching," I said. "It's not deer-hunting season."

"How do you know that?"

"I've been reading up on hunting and trapping regulations. Archery opens October 1. Firearm season opens November 15. There are other things he could be hunting, but not deer."

"What do you want to do? Report him to someone?"

"I think we should, but we need some proof. We should get a photo of the deer in the truck and the license plate number. Can you turn around?"

"Well, we need to turn around since we're going the wrong way. As we drive by, you get a photo of his license plate."

Cooper made a U-turn in the road. By the time we reached the truck, Stanley was already driving; we were directly behind him. I was able to get a clear photo of the truck and license plate, but the deer wasn't visible.

The only problem was that the cell service wasn't working. I kept checking every minute or two. Meanwhile, we continued following Stanley. Not intentionally. We just happened to be going in the same direction.

Finally, I was able to connect with service.

"We must be getting close to civilization—the phone is working," I told Cooper. I looked up poaching in Michigan and found a hotline that accepted calls and texts. I sent a text, including the photo, and typed in the location of the truck and said they had a deer in the truck bed.

"That's all we can do," I said.

Chapter 31

Driving across the Mackinac Bridge the second time was just as exciting as the first. Cooper, feeling braver, drove in the far-right lane closest to the railing. The five-mile drive went fast with so much to look at: the bridge with its two huge towers and suspending cables, the water below us and the distant shore as it grew closer.

"Our cabin is a few miles to the left of the bridge," Cooper said.

I scanned the shore but couldn't make out any details.

"We need to find a grocery store before we check in. The cabin has a kitchen so I can cook," he said.

Using the phone's Yelp service, I found a store. Cooper had a grocery list, but it still took us 45 minutes to find everything he needed.

The cabin was at Mackinaw Mill Creek Campground. The place had so many campsites that we got lost, even using the map the woman at check-in had given us. After circling around twice, we found the right drive and finally our cabin.

"It's so cute," I squealed. The miniature log cabin had a front porch with a built-in bench. Its logs, varnished to a yellowish tawny color, looked new. Knotty pine dominated the interior, giving a rustic impression, but the cabin had all the modern-day amenities I could want, including electricity and plumbing. The main room had a queen-size bed, a sitting area and a kitchenette. There were two doors: one led to a bathroom and the other to a bedroom with bunks.

We hauled in our suitcases and the garbage bags of bedding and linens.

"I'll cook if you make the bed," Cooper offered.

Our own pillows, sheets and blankets combined with the aroma of sautéed onion and garlic gave the cabin a homey feel. We sipped wine as Cooper chopped fresh vegetables and then sautéed them in olive oil with onion and garlic. The mixture would be served over brown rice. He accepted my offer to help with the salad.

"Shall we eat outside?" he asked. Each cabin had a picnic table in its front yard.

"Definitely, but we need to hurry. Daylight is fading."

I carried our plates and silverware outside as Cooper finished cooking. As the sun settled to the west, we enjoyed the homecooked meal. In the distance, we could see the lights of the Big Mac as well as headlights of cars traveling the span.

While the cabins on both sides of us were vacant, a family with noisy kids a few doors down had the same idea as we did and were eating their evening meal at their picnic table. They waved when they saw us. We waved back. Maybe that would be us in a few years.

When cleanup was done, we walked on the beach. We found a bench and sat a while soaking in the night air and watching the headlights progress across the bridge. Luckily, Cooper brought along a flashlight for our walk back.

The next morning, we slept in, delighted at being together. For breakfast, which we ate closer to lunch time, we had Cooper's fried potatoes topped with black beans, tomatoes, avocado and lettuce. Delicious as usual.

The day was spent at Mill Creek Discovery Park just a couple miles away. The park had an operational water-powered sawmill and miles of hiking trails. We had leftovers for dinner, followed by Cooper's famous vegan chocolate-truffle pie. The creamy dessert, made with tofu, was my favorite. Love, love, love it.

"I have one more place for us to go," Cooper told me after dinner.

"Tonight?"

"If you're up for it. Headlands International Dark Sky Park," he said.

"What's a dark sky park?"

"A park where lights aren't allowed. No light pollution. You can see the stars—all of them. It's straight west of here on Lake Michigan. Not too far."

"Let's do it, but if lights aren't allowed, how do we see to get around?"

"You can use flashlights with red filters. And I happen to have one." He rummaged through his suitcase and pulled out a flashlight. It could be used as a regular white-light or switched to red.

Surprisingly, the dark sky park wasn't far from the well-lit Mackinaw City. Our plan was to get to Headlands before dark. There was a parking lot with a half-dozen cars and a sign that explained the rules. A mile-long paved trail led to the dark sky viewing area.

The paved trail, more like a one-lane road, was lined with trees on both sides. Dusk settled in as we started our walk to the beach. Cooper tested the red light. It worked, but didn't seem bright enough.

"That's the idea," he said. "It'll be enough light when it's really dark."

When we got to the water, we walked along the beach a few hundred feet. Traces of the sunset still visible in the western sky helped with out footing. But soon, that wisp of light was extinguished by a low bank of rolling clouds that dashed any hope of seeing a starlit sky.

"It's really dark out here," I said. It may have sounded like an obvious thing to say, but I was surprised by the darkness.

In the far distance, lightning danced across the sky.

"Wow, that's something to see," Cooper exclaimed.

"I'd rather see it from inside, not a mile from our car in total darkness. Maybe we should start back."

Cooper agreed. The dim red-light wasn't enough for us to find the sandy trail from the beach to the pavement. He switched the flashlight to white light, which was so bright it reminded me of the type of spotlight used to shine on prisoners during a prison break. With pavement under our feet, he switched the light back to red.

We discovered the trail had ground-level reflectors that

caught the flashlight's beam to ensure we were heading in the right direction. I tucked my arm around Cooper's arm and matched my stride to his. The canopy of trees blocked the lightning, but the distant rumble of thunder caused our strides to lengthen. Large drops of rain began to fall just as we reached the protection of the Jeep.

"That was close," I said.

"We'll have to come back in better weather," Cooper agreed.

The windshield wipers ran full speed our entire drive back to the cabin. We got drenched dashing from the Jeep to the porch. Inside, we changed to dry clothes and hung the wet ones in the shower. Cooper poured us wine. We cuddled under a blanket on the porch watching the rain obscure the lights of the bridge. The thunderclaps, sometimes near enough to shake the cabin, didn't scare me. I felt protected and safe with Cooper at my side.

When the wine was gone and we were chilled from the damp-night air, we retired to the bed. The storm raged as we found comfort in each other's arms.

Chapter 32

In the morning, my feelings were mixed. Part of me wanted to stay in bed forever with Cooper and part of me wanted to go home to Grams and my fur-family. I felt the ring and knew some day I'd have both.

"We have to check out by ten," Cooper reminded me.

We showered, ate oatmeal with blueberries, stripped the bed and stuffed the sheets, pillows and blankets in the garbage bag for transport. Packing all our stuff in the Jeep didn't take long. At exactly 10 o'clock, we returned the key to the registration desk and picked up our key deposit. Just like that, we were on I-75 heading south. Vacation was over.

"I love getting away, but I love going home even more," I said to Cooper as he drove. As soon as the words were out of my mouth, I remembered that going home meant Cooper would be leaving the following day, and we'd be apart once more. I reached over and took his hand in mine. Our fingers intertwined.

"But as much as I look forward to seeing Grams and the dogs and horses, it's going to be hard to say goodbye to you. I can't wait until you move here," I told him.

Cooper squeezed my hand. "Soon. I'll be here as soon as possible."

Absorbed in our own thoughts, silence descended. Our clutched hands provided me with a sense of intimacy. Cooper's thumb gently rubbed the back of my hand, a soothing feeling that I often craved when we were apart.

My thoughts drifted to the reason Grams had insisted on my being gone for a few days. *Did anyone recognize me in that photo in the newspaper?* I doubted it. If I hadn't known it was me, I wouldn't have known it was me. Plus, I had an alibi: the bachelorette party. I refused to worry about it. Instead, I focused on the now and being with Cooper.

"Do you want to stop anywhere?" Cooper asked me. "Get out and stretch your legs?"

"I'm fine. I'm anxious to get home. I've missed Grams and the dogs."

"Homesick?" he teased.

"Yup. I like home."

"Then we'll keep driving," he replied, giving my hand a squeeze.

"I'm so happy for you both," Grams gushed as we got out of the Jeep. I held out my hand to show off the engagement ring. "Beautiful," she said, giving me a hug. "Was she surprised?" she asked, turning to Cooper.

"I think so."

"Shocked was more like it. I had no idea," I clarified.

The dogs jumped and hovered around us, excited we were home. Cooper tussled with Cody while I bent over and gave Blue a kiss. Buddy barged in for his share of attention as did Shadow. Elvis and Sinatra hung back, waiting their turns.

"Quite the homecoming," Cooper beamed.

"How's Buster? And Bessie?" I asked.

"Buster's good. He's restless and wants out. Bessie and her baby are doing well. Dr. Livingston checked them over and said they're both healthy. He looked at Buster, too, and said he looks good."

"I'm thinking of returning Buster tomorrow," I admitted.

"Good idea," Grams agreed. "Are you hungry? I have a pot of bean stew on the stove and some homemade wheat bread."

"Sounds delicious."

After unloading the Jeep, Grams ordered us to sit at the table while she served us. To celebrate our engagement, she had baked a vegan carrot cake, complete with the word "Congratulations" written in orange frosting.

"You've been busy," Cooper remarked as Grams filled the table with the homemade feast.

"It's too quiet around here without Alison. I cook when I'm lonely," she confessed.

"It's good to be home," I said. "I missed you, too."

While we ate, we told Grams about our adventures in the U.P. She shared stories of when she and her husband had camped on the shores of Lake Superior.

"All I remember is how cold the water was. It took my breath away, and I was only in up to my knees," she said. "I wanted to go swimming, but couldn't. It was just too damn cold."

I insisted on clearing the table. Cooper washed the dishes while I dried, and Grams put things away.

"What do you want to do on your last day in Michigan?" I asked Cooper. "Not that there's much left of the day." The sun was already making its way to the western horizon.

"How about a ride to the river?" he suggested. He even talked Grams into joining us.

"It's been a while since I've been in a saddle," she admitted. "Maybe *too* long."

At the barn, I whistled and the horses came running. We laughed at the sight of Bessie and her baby trailing behind the herd.

"We need a name for the baby," Grams said.

"I still like Fella," I said.

"He *is* a cute little fella," Grams agreed.

"Then he's Fella," I decided.

We saddled the horses. Cooper helped Grams up onto MaryLu as I mounted Dappy. Cooper rode Chester.

"Which way?" Cooper inquired.

"We don't have much time before the sun goes down. Let's just do the usual loop," I said. The loop, which took less than an hour, meant riding down the lane, along the river, through the field and back to the barn.

The horses knew the route and the routine. Chester, who had been Gramps' horse, took the lead. When I spent summers on the farm as a kid, my grandparents bought Dappy for me. Whenever the three of us went for a ride, Dappy and I were always second in line. Grams followed behind me so she could keep an eye on me.

"You go next," I told Grams. Our roles were starting to change.

Now I felt the need to keep an eye on her.

MaryLu balked at being second. I had to hold Dappy back, but both horses did as they were guided to do.

"Can you handle a canter?" Cooper asked Grams after the horses settled down.

"Of course. I'm not *that* old," she retorted with a bit of irritation in her voice.

Cooper nudged Chester with his heels until the horse broke into a gentle canter. Without instruction, MaryLu and Dappy followed his gait. I watched as Grams' body became one with the rhythmic stride. I didn't need to worry about her riding abilities.

The lane was the only part of the loop suitable for running. The path along the river had too many low branches and narrow areas. Plus, the scenery was such that a slow pace gave us time to appreciate the gently moving water, turtles sunning themselves on logs and the occasional blue herons, bald eagles and ducks.

The sun was settling behind the trees as we unsaddled the horses. We turned them loose into the pasture and watched as all three, one by one, kneeled down and then rolled on their back.

Grams joined us for a glass of wine on the porch, but she didn't stay long.

"You two need to be alone," she pronounced. "You have a wedding to plan."

"We've been alone all week. Stay," Cooper coaxed.

She refused and went inside. I heard the TV come on.

"She's happy just knowing we're here," I said.

Since Grams brought it up, I asked if he had anything in mind regarding wedding plans, but I didn't give him a chance to answer. "First, we should pick a date. Then a location. Here? I don't know if Grams would go to California. Or should we elope? Not have a wedding, just get married."

"I vote for eloping, but my folks would be disappointed," Cooper responded. "As for when ... kind of depends on how big a wedding we want and how much time we need for planning. What do want to do?"

"I don't know. I'm still in shock at being engaged. It's only been three days."

"There's no hurry. We don't have to make any decisions tonight," Cooper acknowledged.

The wedding plans were put on hold. Neither of us wanted the day to end. We continued to glide back and forth on the porch swing long after Grams returned to say good night.

"How about a piece of carrot cake?" Cooper asked.

"You know how I love carrot cake," I admitted.

Instead of two pieces, Cooper cut one large piece. We dimmed the lights, sat at a corner of the kitchen table and fed each forkfuls of the sweet, sugary treat.

"I hate to say it, but I have to leave by eight tomorrow morning," Cooper informed me.

"I know. You have a long drive and a plane to catch."

After the cake was gone, we retired to my room for the real dessert.

Chapter 33

I woke to the sound of a knock on the bedroom door.

"Are you guys awake? I thought you had an early day," I heard Grams ask.

In the haze of waking, I glanced at the clock. "We forgot to set the alarm!" I shouted. "We're up now."

"I'm taking a quick shower," Cooper informed me as he rushed to the bathroom.

I took the dogs downstairs and was going to make Cooper breakfast, but Grams had beat me to it. Knowing he was running late, she had packed him a breakfast snack for the road, complete with black coffee.

"Sorry I didn't get you up earlier," she said, "but I didn't want to disturb you."

"We stayed up too late last night," I confessed.

"Does he need help packing?"

"No, he only brought in what he would need this morning. He just has to throw his dirty clothes into his overnight bag." As I spoke, Cooper bounded down the stairs, taking them two at a time. Grams hugged him goodbye and handed him his breakfast. I followed him outside.

"It's been fun," I said. "I'll miss you."

"Me, too. Sorry to have to rush," he said. "I love you. I'll call when I get to O'Hare."

"I love you too." I almost told him to drive safely but didn't. He knew how to drive. "I'll be waiting for your call."

I watched as the Jeep pulled out of the driveway and sped down the road.

Alone again. I looked at my hand. The diamond glittered in

the morning sun and softened the loneliness. Soon, I thought, he'll be back and never need to leave again.

I showered and had a quick breakfast with Grams. "Today my plan is to take Buster back to Stanley, but I'm going to go to the shelter and get caught up there first. I'll pick Buster up on the way out to Stanley's place," I told her.

Cindi, Jason and Carol were sitting in the breakroom when I arrived. Cindi had picked up donuts to celebrate my return.

"I wasn't gone *that* long," I protested.

"Doesn't matter. We missed you," Carol replied.

"You know we look for any excuse to have donuts," Jason added.

"Here's an even better reason to celebrate," I stated, holding up my left hand for everyone to see the engagement ring.

"What is that?" Cindi exclaimed.

"Exactly what it looks like. I'm getting married."

Cindi got up and gave me a hug while Jason asked who I was marrying.

"I didn't even know you were seeing anyone," he said.

"Cooper. He worked for Grams when I first moved here. He moved back to California but we've kept in touch," I explained.

"Do you have a date picked out?" Carol asked.

"No," I said, explaining that I was still in shock about the proposal and hadn't had time to think about wedding details.

Carol congratulated me and said she hoped I wouldn't be moving to California.

I laughed and sat down. Cindi poured me a cup of coffee, and Jason placed a plate with an apple fritter in front of me.

"I'm not going anywhere, and it's good to be back," I said, raising my coffee cup as if making a toast. They followed my lead, and we clinked our cups together.

"A full crew again," Cindi pronounced.

They filled me in on what had happened while I was gone, which wasn't much. I told them about seeing Stanley Jones in the U.P. and reporting him to the DNR.

"I don't know if he recognized me. Cooper talked to him," I explained. "We never heard if the DNR did anything."

I told them my plan was to return Buster to Stanley that day, that Grams' vet had looked at the beagle when he was checking on Bessie and said he looked good.

"Do you want me to go with you?" Jason asked.

"No. I can handle it. If Stanley's not home, I'll just put Buster back in the kennel behind the house. I hate to give him back, but he's his dog."

"Not every home is perfect, and there's not much we can do about it," Cindi offered.

It was close to noon by the time I finished helping Carol clean the kennels and get caught up on paperwork, emails and phone calls.

"I'm going to pick up Buster and have a bite to eat while I'm home," I whispered to Cindi as she listened to someone on her phone. "I'll be back." She waved, acknowledging my message. I waved back.

Grams wasn't home. I wasn't really hungry, so I skipped lunch. The apple fritter so soon after breakfast left me feeling overfed. In the barn, Buster howled and jumped up and down when he saw me.

"You're going home," I told him. "Hope you're happy there. Does he treat you well?"

When we found the beagle caught in the trap, he looked well fed and wasn't scared of strangers. That told me he had been socialized and most likely was treated kindly wherever he lived. Unfortunately, Buster couldn't tell me how he felt about his home or his owner. I snapped a leash onto his collar. We took a short walk around the yard before I opened the passenger door of my car and asked him to jump in. He liked riding in cars.

Stanley's truck was parked in his driveway. I parked behind it, got out and called Buster to get out my door. I had left the leash on him and grabbed it as he jumped out of the car.

"Do you recognize this place?" I asked him. He sniffed the ground and then the air. His tail wagged. I took that as a yes. I also read the happy tail wag as a sign that he was glad to be back. I led him to the door and knocked. After waiting a minute, I knocked again.

I was startled by a voice behind me.

"Hey, Buster, how ya doing?"

I turned and saw Stanley down on one knee and Buster jumping on him.

"The vet said he was ready to be returned," I told him.

Stanley was wearing the same green-and-red plaid shirt he had worn when Cooper and I saw him in the U.P. From the sweaty stench, I doubted if the shirt—or the man—had been washed since then.

"I coulda taken care of the damn dog," he growled without looking at me.

"I was only doing what I thought was in his best interest," I responded.

Stanley turned and stared at me. "*You* thought," he taunted.

"Whatever," I snapped.

Stanley continued to stare. His dark eyes burrowed into my soul. All of a sudden I felt alone and vulnerable. Scared.

"You was up by the quarry," he snarled. "Are you the reason the damn warden came sniffing around?"

"I don't know what you're talking about," I lied. No way would I admit that I saw him. "I'm just bringing your dog back. The county paid his vet bill."

I thought about removing the leash from Buster, but doing so would require getting close to Stanley, and I really didn't want to do that. He could have the leash. I ignored the grizzled old man as I walked past him to my car. My mistake. I should have kept an eye on him. As soon as my back was to him, I heard him move. Then I felt his hand on me. First, a grip on my arm, and then a bear hug from behind. I heard Buster barking.

"Let go of me!" I screamed as I struggled to break his hold. I attempted to elbow him in the gut, but he had me overpowered. I did manage to knock him off balance, and we tumbled to the ground. I tried kicking him, but my feet only kicked air. Then I felt his fist smack my face.

Chapter 34

In my dream, I was being brutalized. Punched. Stomped. Dragged. I woke up trying to scream but, in my terror, my voice was silenced. My mouth opened, but no sound came out. Nothing. Not even a whimper. I gasped for air, choking on my muted screams. Then the realization hit me: it wasn't a dream. The beating had stopped, but what had happened afterward? Where was I?

A bare bulb hung from a ceiling. The low-wattage barely overcame the darkness. I was lying on my back. Underneath me, I felt a blanket; below that, a cold hard floor. Using my hands, I pushed myself into a sitting position.

As my eyes adjusted to the dim light, I looked around me. I was in a basement. A damp, dirty, Michigan basement with a cement floor and walls. An earthy, musty, moldy odor engulfed me. Against one wall stood an antiquated wringer washing machine. Next to it, a clothes drying rack with stuff draped over the rods. There was a staircase and a furnace. Shelves with empty canning jars lined another wall.

My entire body ached, especially my face. I winced with pain as I felt my cheek. What I suspected was dried blood flaked off in my hand. How long had I been lying on the floor? The last thing I remembered was bringing Buster to Stanley Jones and trying to leave. I recalled Stanley grabbing me, and my trying to get free.

I assumed the basement belonged to Stanley. I listened. Silence. What time was it? How did I get in the basement? From the way I felt, Stanley must have dragged me or dumped me down the stairs. My body felt like it had bounced down each step.

Slowly, I got to my feet. Thankfully, no bones appeared broken. I tiptoed over to the stairs, wincing in pain with each step. Moving at a snail's pace and hanging on to the railing to steady myself, I struggled up the stairs to a closed wooden door at the top. Gingerly, I tried to turn the doorknob. It turned, but the door wouldn't budge. I put my ear against the door and listened. Nothing. I felt below the door. There was a slight space, but no light was forthcoming from the other side. Maybe it was night.

I retreated to the blanket, this time pulling it around my shoulders to ward off the damp cool air. I found myself spinning my engagement ring incessantly around my finger. The ring kept Cooper close, which provided an ounce of comfort. I kept my thoughts on the future, not on the possible outcomes of my current situation.

Grams, Cindi and Jason knew I planned to return Buster to Stanley today. They would be looking for me when I didn't return. Cooper was going to call when he got to the airport. What would he do when I didn't answer my phone? Probably figure I had gotten busy at work.

My stomach growled with hunger. I had been stuffed from the morning's donuts when I arrived at Stanley's, which gave me a rough idea of how long I had been there—hours. By the washer, I found a faucet. Turning it on, I rinsed my hands and then cupped my palms to capture the cold water to drink.

On the clothes rack, I found a couple of plaid flannel shirts and a jacket, which I put on. The jacket was too big, but it would help conserve my body heat. I tossed the shirts over to my makeshift bed. They'd come in handy for extra padding or as a pillow or a blanket.

I took a closer look at the basement. It was a single room with no windows. Cobwebs draped in the corners and from the rafters. Next to the drying rack was a wooden box of junk. Near the furnace was a boarded-up area. Perhaps an old coal chute? Before I had time to check it out, I heard the floor creak above me. Then a light shone under the door at the top of the steps.

Was it morning? I wanted to hide, but there was no place to conceal myself. A toilet flushed. I jumped when a motor started, the rumble filling the basement. Investigating, I found what I guessed to be a water pump tucked in darkness behind the furnace.

I looked around for anything I could use as a weapon. Before I could sort through the box of stuff by the clothes rack, the door at the top of the steps opened. I froze in fear as Stanley came down the steps.

"You shoulda kept your nose in your own damn business," he said when he got to the bottom of the stairs. "You're just like that blasted trapper. Meddling. Now, what to do with you."

Since I couldn't physically overtake him, I knew I had to use my wits and talk my way out. "I know you cared about your dog, which is why I was bringing him back to you," I said.

"Buster's a good dog. Joe had no damn right to set that trap where he did."

"You're right. I hate trapping. We're lucky someone found Buster. He could have died in that trap."

"I told Joe that. He laughed at me. Told me I was too sentimental. Him and his damn traps and trophies. I gave him a taste of his own medicine. He won't be laughing at me no more."

What did he mean by that? The answer popped into my head—the trapper who had accidently caught the beagle in a trap had been found dead in his home. He had been shot. Did Stanley kill him? If so, why was he confessing it to me? Was this where I would die?

"I'm sure he deserved whatever you said to him," I said, refusing to show my fear or acknowledge that he had harmed Joe with anything other than words. "I'm hungry. Can I have something to eat?"

Stanley didn't answer. Instead, he turned and stomped up the stairs. My mind raced. I needed a plan. Options ... what were my options? I doubted he was going to let me go. By talking, all I did was buy time.

Could I overtake him? Somehow get around him and escape up the stairs? Could I break down the door?

I went to the box of junk to look for something to use as a weapon. There were a couple of canning jars, some old magazines, a bunch of holey socks, a hoe without a handle, an empty oil can and rags. Could I break the jars and use the broken glass to defend myself?

Upstairs, I heard a TV come on. The floor creaked whenever

Stanley moved about. I didn't know the layout of the house, so I couldn't figure out what he was doing. I took a closer look at the boarded-up wall. Using the old hoe, I pried one of the boards far enough to see a sliver of light shine from behind it. An old window perhaps?

Before I could pry off the board, I heard footsteps overhead near the basement door. I slid the hoe behind the furnace and sat on the blanket in the middle of the room. The door opened and Stanley came down carrying a tray. He set it on the floor next to me. To my surprise, he had brought me a cup of black coffee, toast, and two fried eggs.

"Thank you. That's so nice of you," I cooed.

He didn't say a word. Just turned and left. When he reached the top of the stairs, he turned and looked down at me. "Those eggs are from my ladies."

His comment made me pause. His ladies? Then I recalled the chickens in his backyard. Although I had quit eating eggs, I knew I needed nourishment to keep up my strength. So I ate the eggs. The toast was buttery and the coffee strong. They fueled my resolve to survive.

Another plan came to mind. I would ask to use the bathroom and, once upstairs, somehow escape. While I couldn't overpower Stanley, odds were I could outrun him.

Chapter 35

After gobbling down the meager meal, I savored the hot coffee until the last drop. Being imprisoned infuriated me. Stanley had no right to keep me locked in his basement, but my anger didn't solve anything. I thought of my dog, Blue, and how he must have felt when caged at Kappies Kennels and Sweet's Research. Confused? Scared? My mind turned to all the animals kept restrained against their will, including the cows at Clover Dairy. I shivered at the memory of calves housed away from their mothers in small pens.

My rage fueled the determination to escape. I retrieved the hoe and went back to work prying the wooden boards off the wall. The hoe worked well at first, but its short length didn't yield enough leverage to move the board more than a fraction of an inch. I could almost get my fingers behind the bottom board but couldn't get it to budge. What I wouldn't give for a crowbar or a hammer.

Soon, I really did need to use a bathroom. Would Stanley let me upstairs? If he did, I needed to be prepared to take advantage of whatever situation presented itself, whatever it took. If there wasn't a window in the bathroom to climb out, I'd look for any opportunity to get outside and then run, assuming my body could overlook the bruises and other injuries.

Taking deep breaths for courage, I made my way up the steps and knocked on the door.

"Can I use the bathroom?" I shouted. No answer. I knocked again. "I need to use the bathroom!" I demanded. Finally, I heard footsteps. The door jerked open.

"What?" Stanley said abruptly with a glaring stare. His crankiness had returned.

"Can I use the bathroom?" I asked in a soft demure voice.

He hesitated before answering, making me wonder what he was thinking. "It's that way," he finally said pointing to his left.

My heart started to pound with excitement when I entered the bathroom—there was a window! Small, but large enough for me to squeeze through. When I tried to open it, it wouldn't budge. Looking closely, I saw why. It had been painted over. A heavy coat of white enamel, now a grimy sealant, held the window in place. I remained a prisoner because a window was painted shut.

I peed, flushed the toilet and washed my hands and face. I tried the window again, but it was fruitless. I stared out the glass at freedom. To my astonishment, a truck pulled into the driveway and parked next to the house. It was Jason. What timing! I opened the door to run, but Stanley was waiting for me. He grabbed my arm and held a knife to my throat.

"Make a sound, and I'll stick you like a pig. I'll kill ya both," he whispered. He must have seen Jason's truck, too. "Let's go back to the basement." He pushed me forward. Together we shuffled toward the basement steps. I heard Jason knock at the door. In my mind, I was screaming for help.

But help didn't come.

When I woke, I was in the basement again. I had no idea how long I had been knocked out. The last thing I remembered was Stanley ordering me to the basement and my making the decision to resist. The right side of my throat hurt. Feeling it, I touched what I guessed to be dried blood and an extremely tender spot. He must have stabbed me. Not deep, but enough to draw blood.

I listened. Silence. My face throbbed, as did my back. Stanley must have knocked me out and dragged me down the steps on my backside. My thoughts turned to Jason. Had he heard me? What had Stanley told him? Apparently, he believed whatever Stanley had said, because I hadn't been rescued. Or had Stanley harmed him?

I crawled over to the washing machine and pulled myself up to stand. I turned on the faucet and rinsed my throat, all the while wishing for soap, a clean towel and a bandage.

I wanted to live. I had no idea what Stanley had planned for me, but I knew too much for him to release me. Despite the pain,

I turned my thoughts to escaping and renewed my effort to get the boards off, but I needed more than the head of a hoe.

I took a closer look at the washing machine, hoping to find a removable part that could be used as a wedge. No luck. I looked around the furnace. Nothing usable there either. On one of the shelves behind the canning jars, I spotted a three-foot piece of pipe. Why hadn't I seen it before? Probably because it blended into the shadows. It fit perfectly into the slot where the handle of the hoe once had been. It gave me the leverage I needed to pry the boards off. As I worked, I noticed light no longer showing from behind the boards. The sun must have gone down already.

With the second board off, there was enough space for me to wriggle through. Once outside, I wondered Stanley was. The other side of the house was lit up by an outside light high on his garage. I couldn't see any lights coming from the house. Stanley's truck was in the yard. I assumed he was sleeping. I wondered where my car was. Did I dare look in the garage? No, he wouldn't be stupid enough to leave such evidence on his property.

Tiptoeing, I made my way across the yard to the road. I considered checking Stanley's truck for keys, but decided I didn't want to take the chance of waking the dogs. If they started barking, no doubt Stanley would wake.

Silently, I started to walk down the gravel road. Darkness enveloped me. My entire body screamed in pain, but I didn't listen to it. I kept moving. I wanted to run, but I couldn't see well enough to do more than a slow shuffle. Memories of Cooper's and my walk at Headlands and our wish to see a starlit sky came to me. Such a sky would have been a blessing this night, but cloud cover blocked any stars and moonlight. What I wouldn't give for Cooper's flashlight, but wishing and remembering didn't help. I kept moving. All I wanted to do was put distance between Stanley and me.

When the fear dissipated, my mind turned to trying to remember the layout of the roads and where the nearest house might be. I recalled coming this way when we first picked up Buster, but I didn't recall any houses. Somewhere nearby would be North Country Trail. If I could find it, would I be better off taking the trail? When Stanley discovered I had escaped, he would most likely drive the roads looking for me. The trail might be safer.

The hoot of an owl reminded me that wild animals could be prowling nearby. Black bears, skunks, bobcats, maybe even cougars could be scrounging for their next meal. There was no choice but to ignore the worrisome thoughts and continue trudging down the road. I wondered about the time. How long before the sun would come up?

Chapter 36

I decided I'd be safer on the North Country Trail after all. When Stanley discovered me missing, I pictured him running to his old beat-up pickup and driving around looking for me. The lack of food, my beaten and bruised body and the mental strain all contributed to a feeling of total exhaustion. No way would I find the trail in the dark. I was running on reserve energy, and it, too, was winding down. I had never felt so depleted. I could go no farther. Not one more step. I crumpled into a heap behind a big tree a few feet off the road. In the dark, my right hand felt for the engagement ring. Feeling the band brought memories of Cooper, which brought me comfort. A rustling of leaves caused a moment of concern about snakes, bears and Stanley, but fatigue won and I slept.

The next thing I knew, my face was being licked by Buster.

"Ya didn't get far," Stanley mocked.

I thought I was having a nightmare. In desperation, I tried to wake, only to realize it wasn't a dream. Stanley had found me.

"Ya think I'm dumb? I knew Buster would lead me straight to ya. Git up." He waved a gun toward my face. A gun?

Numb to the situation, I meekly followed his order. Using the tree to steady myself, I stood up. Beside me, Buster executed a three-legged happy dance.

"Move," Stanley ordered, waving his gun in the direction he wanted me to go.

The light of day was settling into the recesses of the forest as we began to walk down the road in the direction from which I had come. Buster walked beside me, his tail wagging. He had no idea what he had done.

Stanley's truck was parked on the side of the road. He picked up Buster and gently placed him in the bed of the pickup. He ordered me to open the driver's door and get in. When I ignored him, he grabbed my arm and shoved me against the truck.

"Open the damn door and git in." I did what he wanted. "Now git your damn ass over," he demanded. I scooted over. "Put on the seatbelt." I did as I was told, knowing the seatbelt would hinder any attempt to escape.

He got in and started driving. I expected him to take me back to his house, to return me to the basement dungeon, but we were headed in the opposite direction.

"Where are we going?" I asked.

He ignored my question. I wondered if he had a plan or if he was just driving. I didn't ask again. I wasn't familiar with all the backroads of the county, so I had no idea where we were or where he might be taking me.

He turned onto a paved road. The street sign was hidden by overgrown tree branches so I couldn't read it. A few cars passed us going in the opposite direction.

"Don't try nothing," he said as if reading my mind.

"Like what? Jumping out when you're driving 50 miles an hour? I'm not stupid either." Although I will admit, the thought of jumping had occurred to me.

We both saw it at the same time—a police car traveling in the opposite direction. I turned to see if the officer might slam on his brakes and do a U-turn. To my surprise, I saw brake lights.

"What ya looking at?" Stanley shouted as he looked in his rearview mirror. "Damn, what did ya do?"

"I didn't do anything." I could only wish I had telepathic powers. Within seconds, I heard a siren.

"Keep your mouth shut," he demanded as he steered the truck to the side of the road and brought it to a stop. "Say a word and the cop is dead, and so are you." He put the gun under his seat and reached over to poke my arm with his index finger as he spoke. "Not a word or you're dead."

I believed him. My heart raced in anticipation. Something was going to happen. Buster was barking. Stanley rolled down his window and shouted at him to be quiet. The barking stopped.

We waited. The time it took the officer to walk up to the window seemed like forever.

"Do you know why I pulled you over?" the officer asked.

Stanley shook his head no. "I have no idea."

"You have a headlight out. Can I see your registration and license please?"

Although they were no longer needed, Stanley hadn't turned off his headlights. What luck. My thoughts jumbled with possibilities. Scream? Run? Attack Stanley? How fast could he retrieve the gun? In the end, I did nothing. I sat there and kept quiet, just like he had instructed.

After looking over the paperwork, the officer told Stanley to get the headlight fixed.

"I surely will, officer. I surely will," he said as he took back the registration and license.

The cop told us to have a good day and left. Stanley turned to me, "Damn, I thought he had us. We did good," he said.

This time I didn't answer. I was out of words. Out of ideas. I couldn't believe the cop walked away. Didn't he notice I looked like hell? Like I had spent the night in the woods? Like I hadn't brushed my teeth or hair in days? Hadn't I been reported missing?

Stanley started the engine and eased the truck out onto the road. The possibility of escape or rescue evaporated.

"S'not your day," Stanley said as if reading my mind. He laughed. "Not your day," he taunted as he leaned over, pulled the gun from below his seat and laid it on his lap.

I turned and looked out the back window of the cab. Buster was resting on a burlap bag and the police car was following us.

"Don't get any damn ideas," Stanley said as he caressed the gun with his right hand.

All of a sudden out of nowhere, a whitetail deer appeared and darted in front of the truck. Stanley swerved and barely missed the animal. Whitetails travel in herds and two more deer dashed across the road right in front of us. There was no avoiding one of them. It slammed into the front of the truck and flipped onto the hood. As the truck jerked to a stop, I unclipped the seatbelt, opened the door and ran. The cop car was still behind us. He, too, had seen the deer and was stopping.

"Help!" I screamed as I ran to police car.

He got out, gun drawn.

"Help! He kidnapped me!" I shrieked. I held my arms up. "Please, help me!"

"Get behind the car," he ordered as he turned his attention to the truck.

As I ducked behind his still-running car, I heard a single gunshot. I then heard the officer calling for backup.

"Stay put," he told me.

Soon I heard sirens, and then another gunshot.

Chapter 37

Stanley was wrong. Turned out it *was* my day.

The first gunshot I had heard was Stanley killing himself. Relief flooded over me after the officer told me what had happened. It was over. There was no doubt that Stanley intended to kill me. He had no choice. He had all but admitted to me that he had shot the trapper. If he let me go, he knew I'd go straight to the authorities. Although I never admitted it, he knew I was the reason he got hassled in the U.P. He was right—he wasn't dumb, just stupid.

The second shot I heard was the officer killing the deer. Such kismet—a deer died and, in doing so, saved my life. Was it one of the deer who escaped from a canned hunt where I cut the fencing? Was it just coincidence that a deer saved my life when I was on a crusade to help deer? Could it be karma? Were bigger forces at work than what could be seen? God? There was no way to know, but whatever was behind the fortunate incident, I was thankful. Thankful to be free. Thankful to be alive.

Buster limped up to me as I waited by the police car. He had either been thrown from the back of the pickup or jumped out. I didn't know if it happened when Stanley swerved to miss the first deer or when he hit the second deer. The poor baby was subdued, not his usual happy self. I wondered if he knew Stanley had died. Other than the slight limp, he seemed okay. His days of riding in the bed of a pickup were over.

Despite my protests, an ambulance was called to take me to the hospital. "All I need is a shower and food," I insisted, but nobody listened. They refused to let me take Buster too.

"Take him to the county shelter," I directed. "I work there. They'll make sure he sees a vet."

They let me use a phone to call Grams. All she did was cry when she heard my voice.

"I was so worried," she said between sobs.

"I'm okay, but they're insisting I go to the hospital to be checked over," I said. "Can you pick me up there?"

I asked her if Cooper knew I had been missing. She said he did and was probably inflight returning to Michigan as we spoke. After reassuring Grams that I was okay, I called Cooper's cell and left him a message.

Next, I called Cindi. She wasn't nearly as emotional as Grams, but close. I told her I knew Jason had been looking for me, that I had been in Stanley's house when he stopped by.

"You're kidding me. He told me he thought Stanley was lying when he said you had dropped off the dog and left."

"He held a knife to my neck. He said if I screamed I'd be dead," I explained, not giving her all the details, they could wait until later. "Any idea where my car is? Or my purse or cell phone?"

"No. We've been looking for you, but you just disappeared. The car too."

"It must be somewhere near Stanley's. Did you know he's dead?" She hadn't heard the news. "Jason needs to go get Stanley's other dogs and his chickens. Did you know he had chickens? Ask him to look for my car while he's there," I told her. "Oh, and they're going to be dropping off Buster. He was with us. Hold him for me. I want him."

She laughed. "Glad to hear you're feeling well enough to give orders. You must be okay. I'll see you at the hospital."

"Three calls are enough," the paramedic told me as he took back his phone. "Lay back and rest."

"Do you have anything to eat?" I asked. He gave me a granola bar.

The ambulance beat Grams and Cindi to the hospital. I wasn't there long. They cleaned a couple of cuts. Nothing needed stitches. They instructed me to take over-the-counter pain medication if needed.

"I just want to go home and shower and eat. Then sleep in my own bed," I said.

And that's exactly what happened.

While I showered, Grams heated up some soup and made me a salad and a sandwich. While I ate, I told her and Cindi what had happened.

"I thought I was a goner," I admitted. "I got lucky."

Jason called and said he was on his way to Stanley's place to pick up the dogs. "I heard you were in the house when I stopped by Stanley's," he said.

"I was. I saw you. In my head I was screaming at you," I joked.

"Maybe I heard you, because I knew he wasn't telling the truth, but he insisted you had dropped of the dog and left. I'm so sorry. I should have done more."

"Like what?" I asked. "You did what you could at the time. I'm sure you would have been back sooner or later."

"But later could have been too late. I blew it."

I tried to ease his guilt, but he refused to listen. I invited him to visit in the morning. "We'll hash it out then. Now I'm going to eat and then sleep," I said.

As soon as I hung up from talking to Jason, the phone rang again. This time it was Cooper. Due to a problem with the airplane, he was on a layover in Denver where he would be spending the night.

"I'll be there sometime tomorrow. How are you? What happened?"

Grams nudged me and pointed at the food. "Let me talk to him," she instructed.

I assured Cooper that I was fine and told him that Grams wanted to talk to him. I handed her the phone. I listened as she told him that I needed to quit talking and start eating. She laughed, and I wondered what he had said to her.

"Let me in on the joke," I begged after she got off the phone.

"He just said he knew you were okay if you wanted to eat."

"It's been days since I ate," I said in defense.

"You weren't even gone two days," she stressed.

"And all I ate in that time was two fried eggs and toast. Oh, and a granola bar the ambulance driver gave me."

Cindi started laughing, which got Grams laughing. I realized the absurdity of the situation. I had been kidnapped, could have died, and here I was arguing with them about food. Laughter beat tears.

When Cindi left, she told me to take the rest of the week off. We hugged. "You had me worried. I'm thankful you're okay."

Chapter 38

Exhausted, I expected to sleep long and hard, but the rest I craved eluded me. Instead, nightmares plagued my mind. A jumbled mix, as if everything that had happened in the last two days had been put in a blender and rearranged, but the one constant was fear. Being hunted. Gunshots. Running. Claustrophobia. Darkness. Confusion. Helplessness. Being chased by deer. By dogs. By something unknown.

I tried to scream but could only whimper. When I clawed my way back to reality, I turned on the bedside lamp. The dogs were sleeping on the floor, except for Blue. He snored by my feet. The normalcy consoled me. I was home. I was safe. I looked at the clock. I had been in bed for less than an hour. If I had my cell phone, I would have called Cooper. In the bathroom, I found some Tylenol PM. I took two and lay back down, leaving the light on, hoping the brightness would curb the night terrors. The drugs worked their magic. I slept without remembrance of what went on in my head.

When I woke, the dogs had deserted me. No doubt with the help of Grams. I showered, savoring the hot water as it cascaded over me and loosened my stiff muscles. I delighted in the rose-blossom-scented shampoo. But as much as I tried to wash away the events of the last two days, they were Velcroed to my soul.

For some reason, the scene that haunted me the most was Stanley's truck hitting the deer. The sudden appearance of the animal, the impact, its flipping onto the hood and windshield, the thud of flesh as it collided with metal played in a loop inside my head.

I refused to let the scene replay and shook my head. I flipped my thoughts to happier things: Cooper, my wedding. I kissed the engagement ring. It had become my talisman, my lucky charm that brought good fortune. I dressed and limped downstairs. To my surprise, Jason was sitting at the kitchen table having coffee with Grams. He got up and greeted me with a gentle hug.

"Good morning sleepy head. We were beginning to wonder if you were getting up today," he teased.

"What time is it?" I asked, surprised that I hadn't paid attention to the alarm clock next to my bed.

"Almost ten," Grams said as she poured me a cup of coffee.

"I was beat," I reasoned.

"I brought donuts," Jason said pushing a box of the sugary treats over to me.

"Just like the last time I saw you. Coffee and donuts," I remarked. And, just like that last get-together in the breakroom at the shelter, I grabbed an apple fritter.

Jason had good news. "Your car was in Stanley's barn. Your purse and phone too," he said pointing to the counter. My purse sat next to my phone, which was plugged into the charger.

"Thank God. I've missed my phone."

"I brought Buster back too. He's in the barn."

"Oh, good. How many other dogs did he have?"

"Four, all beagles. They're at the shelter."

"And the chickens?"

"They have food and water. I wasn't sure what to do with them."

I looked at Grams as I took a sip of the hot coffee.

"We used to have chickens," she admitted. "I can help catch them."

"Should we bring them here?" I asked. Jason and Grams laughed. "What?" I asked.

"No matter what it is, you always want to bring it home," Jason replied.

"So?"

"It would be nice to have chickens again," Grams admitted. "But this time we won't be eating them."

With that settled, I told Jason about my suspicions regarding Stanley. "He told me he had argued with the guy who owned the trap that Buster had been caught in. He all but confessed to shooting him."

Jason held up his hand to stop me from saying more. "Sheriff McCarthy wants you to come to the station to give a formal report about what happened. After that, we can talk about it."

"Can't I just tell you what happened?"

"No, you need to talk to the sheriff."

"When?"

"You need to do it while it's still fresh. How about now?"

As much as I dreaded it, I agreed to the interview. "Let's get it done ... after I finish this," I said, holding up the half-eaten fritter.

Jason asked if I wanted a ride to pick it up my car, but also offered to have someone else drive it to the farm.

"I can drive," I said.

"How about I take you to see the sheriff and then take you to get the car afterwards?"

I took two aspirin to dull the aches and we were off.

I spent two hours drinking coffee and detailing my ordeal to Sheriff McCarthy and Jason. Since Stanley had committed suicide when confronted by the officer, the session seemed irrelevant. He was dead and couldn't be held accountable for the physical abuse or for keeping me imprisoned.

"Does any of this matter?" I asked.

"Since Stanley is dead, not really, but if it'll help us close the book on the homicide of Joe DeYoung, then it's definitely worth it," the sheriff responded.

I did my best to describe everything that happened and answered all their questions.

"Was it just a fluke that you saw him in the U.P.?" Jason asked.

"Yes. Just a coincidence. I was surprised to see him and didn't think he recognized me, but apparently he did."

"What are the odds?" Jason questioned.

I didn't have an answer. What were they thinking? That I followed him up north? I was starting to get irritated. "I don't know. Are we almost done? I've told you everything I know. I'm getting tired," I sniped.

"We can be done," Sheriff McCarthy said. He thanked me for coming in and told me if they had any other questions, they'd be in touch. "Rest. Take it easy for a few days and, again, thanks for coming in."

"I don't know what else I can tell you. We've covered it pretty thoroughly," I said.

Jason butted in. "I'm taking her to get her car. Then she'll go home and take it easy."

When we were back in Jason's truck, he turned to me and apologized again for not doing more to rescue me.

"Jason, how could you have known I was in the house? You did all you could do. There's nothing to apologize for. Got it? Nothing to be sorry for."

"Okay. I just want you to know that I'm sorry for what happened to you."

"I know. I know. Take me to my car. I appreciate you finding my car."

My car had been moved from the barn to the driveway and was parked in almost the exact spot where I had left it. I sat in the truck and stared at the house.

"Can we go in?" I asked.

"What?"

"Can I go in the house?"

"Why would you want to do that?"

"Just to look around. I had nightmares last night. Maybe if I saw the basement again it wouldn't haunt me."

"Sure, we can go in. It isn't locked. We were here last night looking for anything we could find about next of kin."

"He has that brother in the U.P."

"Stuart. Yeah, I found his telephone number and called him already," Jason said as he led the way to the house.

Jason held the door open, but I hesitated before entering.

"You don't have to do this," he said.

"Yes, I do. I need to face my fear."

Jason offered me his hand. I accepted and stepped over the threshold.

"Are you okay?" he asked.

I nodded.

In the bathroom, I pointed to the window that was painted shut. "This is where I was when I saw you pull in the driveway. If I could have gotten the window open, your timing would have been perfect."

Jason inspected the window and tried to open it. He couldn't budge it either.

From there we went to the basement. The smell hit me as soon as I went through the door. That musty earthy odor would be forever linked to Stanley's house. Jason followed me as I started down the stairs. I stopped about halfway down debating if I truly wanted to revisit the hellhole. As if reading my mind, Jason put his hand on my back and said, "I'm right behind you."

I took a deep breath and forced myself to continue downward. The light from upstairs was enough for me to see where the bulb hung from the ceiling. I pulled the chain and the lightbulb flicked to life.

The first thing I noticed was that the boards had been nailed back in place. "That was where I got out," I said, pointing to the walled-up window. "Stanley must have nailed the boards back up." The hoe and pipe were still on the floor. "Can I take this?" I asked grabbing the hoe.

"I don't see why not," Jason replied.

I wandered around just looking. The furnace. The shelves. I picked up the blanket and shirts from the floor and put them on the washing machine.

"At least he left the light on for me, and he didn't tie me up. It could have been worse." I shivered at the thought of what could have been.

"Being tied up down here in the dark would have been terrifying," Jason agreed.

"He didn't know what to do with me. I think he acted on impulse when he grabbed me, and once he had me locked up down here, he just didn't know what to do with me."

"Could be," Jason agreed.

"He wasn't all bad--he cooked me breakfast ... and he cared about his dogs."

Jason laughed. "He had two redeeming qualities. He fed his prisoner and he liked dogs," he joked.

I snapped my head around and looked at him.

"What? I'm agreeing with you. He liked dogs," Jason said. "It should be in his obituary."

"Stanley Jones, who loved dogs, was a killer and a kidnapper," I joked.

"Sounds like a good first line," Jason teased.

"This is even better: Stanley Jones loved dogs and was a killer and a kidnapper. He also loved his chickens, who he referred to as his little ladies."

"Little ladies?" Jason repeated with a chuckle.

"Yup, the eggs he served me were from his *ladies*. That's what he told me."

Being there with Jason and hearing him laugh helped me relax. The basement was losing its hold. "Thanks for letting me come down here. I'm feeling better. It's just a basement."

"It's just a basement," Jason repeated. I reached out and gave him a hug. He hugged me back. "You're safe," he whispered in my ear.

His kindness brought tears to my eyes.

Jason told me there was something upstairs he wanted me to see. I followed as he led me to the kitchen. The table, piled with stacks of papers and magazines, had just enough room for one place setting. I imagined Stanley all by himself, eating his meals surrounded by piles of junk he couldn't throw out.

"I didn't go through all the papers, but what I did see surprised me," Jason stated.

"How so?" I asked.

"Look," he said pointing.

On the top of one pile was a magazine from the Humane Society of the United States. The mailing label had Stanley's name and address on it. Next in the pile was an envelope from PETA—People for the Ethical Treatment of Animals.

"What the hell?" I asked Jason as I leafed through literature from numerous animal-welfare and anti-hunting organizations.

"Your guess is as good as mine," he replied. "Apparently he was an animal lover. I'm assuming he was angry at Joe DeYoung, not just because Buster was caught in his trap, but because he hated trapping. Maybe he hated hunting too. Joe's house had a trophy room with mounts from around the world. He even had the head of a rhinoceros. Even I found it disturbing."

"But I thought Stanley was hunting in the U.P." I thought back to what Stanley's neighbor had told me. Did he say Stanley was hunting or did he just say Stanley was in the U.P.? I couldn't say for sure either way.

"When I talked to his brother, he said Stanley had just been there," Jason informed me. "They had a run-in with a game warden who questioned them about poaching, but they hadn't been hunting. Stanley didn't hunt."

"Wow, if that's true, I sure had Stanley pegged wrong. We might have to change his obituary," I joked.

Jason continued. "Stuart told me they had picked up a deer they found dead on the side of the road. He has a wolf sanctuary and uses road kill to feed his animals."

"A wolf sanctuary?" I echoed.

"In Michigan it's illegal to own wolves or wolves crossbred with dogs," Jason explained. "When the state passed the law, some people got rid of their wolf-dogs. Stuart got a permit from the state so he could take them in."

"I don't know what to think," I said as I continued to look through the stacks of magazines. Most were from animal rights organizations. "I'm stunned."

"I'm guessing Stanley didn't mean to kill Joe. I'm beginning to think Stanley had a quick temper and acted before he thought. He was mad at Joe, and if Joe taunted him.... Probably the same with kidnapping you. Who knows what he planned to do. We'll never know."

"I'll tell you one thing. I feel lucky," I said. "He was backed into a corner. I couldn't tell what he was thinking, but it wasn't good."

I looked through the rest of the tiny house. Stanley definitely had his share of junk—there were boxes and piles of stuff everywhere. The floor of the bedroom had heaps of clothes. I doubted if the washing machine in the basement got much use. The living room had a saggy chair across from a TV and a couch. A blanket was draped over the couch and the cushions were stacked with stuff.

"Let's go, I've seen enough," I told Jason.

As the door clicked closed behind us, I felt lighter. Stanley Jones was an enigma, a puzzle that couldn't be solved now that he was dead.

"Maybe he just had a short fuse and his temper got the best of him," I said. "What did his brother say about him?"

"Not much. He plans on coming here to figure out the estate. He didn't have any other family."

"Now I feel sorry for him. The guy was probably going to kill me, and I feel bad that he had a lonely, crappy life."

"Sounds like you need a therapist, Alison."

"Thanks."

"No really. You've been through a lot. It wouldn't hurt to talk to a professional."

"I'll think about it."

"While we're here, we should check on the chickens," Jason said.

We walked out back to the fenced pen. The chickens wandered around scratching in the dirt and grass.

"I know nothing about chickens," I confessed.

"Me neither," Jason revealed.

"Good thing Grams does."

Inside the shed was a garbage can filled with chicken feed. Jason scooped some into a bucket. The chickens came running when they heard him pour the food into two pans inside their pen.

"The *ladies*," I said. "I wonder if they have names."

Chapter 39

Getting in my car and driving away from Stanley's gave me the best feeling. Freedom. Safety. I waved to Jason. How fortunate I was to have such an exceptional friend and coworker. I rolled down the window and inhaled the crisp autumn air. It eased the overwhelming sense of confinement I had felt in the basement.

Pulling into Grams' driveway, I noticed a strange car parked by the house. Then I noticed the Illinois license plate. Cooper! I ran inside. He was seated at the kitchen table with Grams. He greeted me with a hug and a kiss.

"You made it," I said.

"I almost have the drive memorized," he joked. "How are you?"

"A little stiff and sore, but other than that, I'm okay. I got my car back. Just spent a couple hours telling my story to the sheriff, which was nauseating, but I survived. I'm so sorry you had to come back, but I'm glad you did."

"I can't stay long. I booked a return flight for tomorrow afternoon."

"Tomorrow?"

"Sorry. My PO isn't being too sympathetic, and I can't afford to piss him off. But we have today."

Since the weather was gorgeous, we decided to spend the late afternoon at the Ludington State Park, which was just north of town.

"Are you sure you're up to it," Cooper asked.

"As long as we go slowly and I take a couple more aspirin, I'll be okay."

Between the tourists being gone for the summer and the fact

that it was a weekday, the parking lot at the park was empty. We wandered down to the beach. The sky was a brilliant blue and the lake adopted the color. Seagulls skimmed the calm water looking for their next meal. Other gulls danced with the small waves as they fished from the beach. Looking at the horizon, it was hard to tell where sky stopped and water began.

"Are you up to walking to the lighthouse?" Cooper asked. The Big Sable Lighthouse was a two-mile walk one way on a flat access road.

"I'm game to try."

"We can turn around whenever you want," Cooper said.

As we started, Cooper asked me to tell him about what had happened. So, I regaled him with my tale, trying to downplay my fear. He listened, asked a few questions, and when I finished, he started giving me advice, which I didn't want to hear. My patience had been depleted with the sheriff's interview.

"Telling me to be careful means nothing. I'm always cautious," I snapped, after he scolded me for not being careful. He didn't back down.

"You're too trusting. You keep putting yourself in dangerous situations. You need to stop and think about what you're doing," he said in a calm voice. "I don't want to lose you."

"I *do* think," I said, stopping mid-thought. He was right, and I didn't want to argue. Not on our only day together. "I'm sorry. You're right. I get caught up in the moment. I've always felt invincible. But I admit, this time I was scared. Really scared."

He apologized. I apologized. We vowed not to discuss it anymore. Instead, we enjoyed the day and our time together.

The lighthouse wasn't open for tours, but seeing the tower loom against the blue sky brought a discussion of what it would have been like to be a keeper of the lighthouse before automation. Lonely? Boring? It helped keep the conversation light and less annoying but, inevitably, our talk returned to animal issues. Sitting on a log overlooking the lake and listening to the melodic lapping of the waves, we discussed the morality of breaking laws that we thought were unjust.

"Slavery was once legal, and helping free slaves was a crime," I offered, trying to rationalize my behavior.

"True, but you have to be willing to risk your life and your freedom, and I'm not willing to take that gamble anymore," Cooper declared.

"But I get so damn mad when I see what's being done to animals, I just want to scream," I said, my voice getting louder to match my frustration.

"I know, believe me, I know. Killing contests are becoming my pet peeve, and I feel the same way you do."

"Killing contests? I don't know what they are."

"Contests to see who can kill the most animals in a certain time period. There are prizes for the most animals killed, sometimes for the biggest animal killed. Usually they're for predators like coyotes, bobcats and foxes, but I've seen them for squirrels too. Any animal considered a nuisance," Cooper explained.

"Contests? It's madness. When will it end?"

"Not in our lifetime," Cooper said. "But that doesn't justify breaking the law. Look at Stanley. He went overboard. If he hadn't killed himself, he'd probably be spending the rest of his life in prison. You don't want that."

"You're right," I said standing up. We continued the debate all the way back to the parking lot.

Grams had offered to cook us dinner if we promised to be home at a reasonable hour. We told her we'd be back before dark, and we were.

"It's almost ready," she advised when I asked if we had time to do chores before eating. I was famished so I asked what she was making. "Harvest stew. I found a few more veggies in the garden. This is the last batch. I promise," she said.

"Not a problem."

Cooper waited for me outside and helped feed the barn animals. After taking Buster for a walk, I bought him into the house instead of locking him back up in the stall.

"Are you planning on keeping him?" Cooper asked as he washed his hands at the kitchen sink.

"Meg wanted to adopt him. After what happened to her, I'm tempted to keep him as a way to remember her."

"How many animals do you have time for? Not to mention the expense."

"I don't know," I replied honestly.

"We talked about starting a sanctuary," Grams chimed in. "Maybe the time has come. We could become a nonprofit. Donations could help with the expenses."

The discussion picked back up after dinner while we sat on the porch.

"What do we need to do to become a nonprofit?" I asked Cooper.

He didn't know all the details, but knew there was a lot of paperwork and a filing fee. He offered to look into it. "What types of animals do you want to work with? You should specialize. Like farm animals or rescued research animals or dogs."

"Since we already have cows and horses, farm animals are a given. Every farm has dogs and cats, so they seem a perfect fit too."

"There're a lot of details to work out. We'd need a presence on social media––and a name," he added.

"I've been giving the name some thought," I said. "How about the Thomas Blue Sanctuary? We'd be paying tribute to Gramps and my son and to Blue, since he's the one who got it all started."

Grams and Cooper both thought the name was good, but apparently not perfect since they started coming up with other names. Blue Sky Sanctuary. Blue Pearline Sanctuary. Thomas' Safe Haven.

When we couldn't agree on a name, Grams suggested we think on it and excused herself to give us some time alone. We stayed on the porch until the night chill convinced us to go inside. On our way upstairs, we said our goodnights to Grams who was watching TV.

Snuggling with Cooper gave me security, and I slept well. Morning came too quickly. Before I knew it, we were saying goodbye again.

"Stay out of trouble," he joked as he got in the car. "I'll call when I get to the airport."

I promised I'd answer.

Chapter 40

Grams left for a garden club luncheon shortly after we said our goodbyes to Cooper, which left me alone. What an oddity to have a day to myself. My body still ached. I regretted hiking the afternoon before, but the day had been too beautiful not to be outside.

I decided on a hot bath with Epsom salts to ease my pain. The warmth of the water relaxed me to the point of napping, but instead of my usual nighttime drama, I had a vivid dream.

A fawn came to me. The baby deer stood by a hedgerow and stared in my direction. She hesitantly took a few steps toward me. I remained still as she came closer. I could almost reach out and stroke her soft brown fur speckled with white spots. With innocent inquisitiveness, she sniffed the air. She appeared as mesmerized by me as I was by her. I gazed at her in amazement and wondered why she was alone.

"Where's your momma?" I whispered.

Upon hearing my voice, the fawn bolted and disappeared into the forest. I regretted talking to her. After she was gone, I woke up.

The dream felt more like a vision, and it didn't fade away. When I finished my bath, I asked Google what was meant by a fawn appearing in a dream. I learned that a deer is a noble symbol representing the spiritual aspect of life.

> Deer like to hide, and they only come out from hiding when necessary. A deer in your dream can symbolize a type of awakening, but likely a spiritual awakening. A deer symbolizes the opening of your heart. Often, a deer

portrays good news and good luck. If you saw a baby deer in the dream, it predicts a financial beginning and achievement of your life goals. In other words, seeing a baby deer represents success and wealth. To see a fawn portrays your vulnerability and innocence.

The interpretation of the dream felt accurate. Learning about trapping and canned hunts had been an awakening for me. I also felt as if my heart was opening more to Cooper. If a baby deer predicted a financial beginning and the achievement of life goals, then I was on the right track starting a nonprofit animal sanctuary. The last line—that a fawn portrays vulnerability and innocence—reminded me of what Cooper said he thought of me. That I was too trusting.

I felt the dream about the fawn both confirmed and urged the continuation of my nighttime visits to the hunting preserves.

Although I promised Grams and Cooper that I wouldn't cut any more fences, I knew I had to do one more. I felt a kinship to the whitetail deer, and I had a debt to pay for the one who sacrificed her life so I could escape from Stanley. Part of me thought it was a crazy, stupid idea, but it felt like divine instruction.

Once again, I found myself researching hunting preserves in Michigan. The one that caught my eye was named Blue Sky Whitetail Sanctuary. First, Blue Sky was one of the names that had been tossed out in our brainstorming session for our sanctuary's name. Second, I despised the word *sanctuary* used in the name of a canned-hunting business. It made the place sound pristine and peaceful. A better name would be Blood Sky Killing Club.

I thought about a recon visit, but the place was a two-hour drive away. I decided it would have to be done in one trip. Leave early enough to check it out in daylight. Hang low until night fell and then return to do the deed. I also decided there was no time like now.

I Googled the address and found a satellite photograph of the place. I couldn't tell for sure where the fence was. There were several buildings—some most likely cabins for the hunters. On their website, they offered overnight packages with guided hunts and guaranteed kills. There were open fields and large tracts of wooded land. The operation looked remote without any close neighbors. Ripe for the picking ... or clipping.

My brain kicked in. First, I needed an alibi for Grams about where I would be tonight. The only explanation that sounded feasible was to tell her I was going to visit Sara in Grand Haven, and I really could go visit my childhood friend. My arrival time would just be a little later than expected. When I called Sara, she was excited at the idea of my visit.

"This is so perfect. My friends are having a baby shower for me Saturday afternoon. You can come with me," she exclaimed with delight.

I had walked right into that one, and there was no way out. "Really? What timing."

"They'll be so excited to meet you," she claimed.

"Great. I have an appointment at seven tonight that shouldn't take long. I'll probably be there by nine."

She was fine with the late-night arrival and was already making plans.

"Whatever you want to do is fine by me," I told her when she questioned how I wanted to spend the rest of the day. "Just spending time with you is all I want."

I packed two bags: a suitcase for the stay with Sara and a backpack with my camouflage outfit. I placed the backpack, along with the bolt cutters, in the back seat of my car before Grams returned home.

To be at Blue Sky at dusk, I calculated I should leave about four o'clock. With a plan in place, I was restless with nervous energy.

I hung out in the yard with the dogs for a while, letting them get used to Buster. Luckily, introducing him to the pack was easy. They had already seen each other from a distance, and their smells mingled in the yard. The face-to-face introduction was just a formality.

I took the dogs for a walk and noticed the ground under the apple trees along the lane was littered with ripened fruit. I went back to the barn for burlap bags. One I filled for deer bait that I put in the car. The other one was for me. The day had a chill to it, so when I got back to the house I baked an apple crisp. Then I made a cup of tea and ate a huge slice of the dessert for lunch.

All the time I waited for Cooper to call. When the phone finally rang, I answered it after one ring.

"You still safe at home?" he joked.

"I am. Just sitting here waiting for your call." His remark made me feel both guilt and defiant. "How was the drive?" I asked diverting the subject with small talk.

The drive had been without incident. His flight was on time, which meant he didn't have time to chat. I told him I was going to Sara's but would be home Saturday evening. We agreed to talk when I got back to the farm.

Playing solitary on the computer occupied my time until Grams came home. "I'm bored," I pouted. "I'm not used to having time on my hands."

"Smells good in here. Have you been cooking?"

"Baking. An apple crisp."

"Is there any left?"

Her comment made me laugh. "Of course. You think I ate it all? Do you want a piece?"

She did. I heated more water for tea and scooped out two servings of the crisp. While we relaxed with our afternoon snack, I told her of my decision to drive to Grand Haven to see Sara. "It's just an overnighter. She's having a baby shower Saturday afternoon that she wants me to go to. I'll be back tomorrow evening."

"Are you feeling up to the drive?"

"I soaked in the tub this morning. That felt good. I still have aches, but I'm going to ache no matter where I am."

"When are you leaving?"

"Soon. I'm already packed. I'll stop on the way to buy a gift."

I felt a twinge of guilt about leaving and an even bigger twinge about breaking my promise to Grams. My justification was that it had been a promise she shouldn't have demanded.

Chapter 41

The face of the innocent fawn held center stage in my mind while the promises to Grams and Cooper faded into the background. The two-hour drive sped by. I had memorized the directions to Blue Sky, along with how to get to Grand Haven. When I was getting close, I pulled over to the side of the road. With no houses or traffic in view, I unzipped the backpack and donned the wig, ball cap and fake glasses. I slipped the jacket over my T-shirt, and my disguise was complete.

There wasn't a sign for the so-called sanctuary, but the gate and fencing indicated I was in the right place. The website said they had 200 acres. I drove the roads around the business, keeping an eye out for the telltale fencing. Unfortunately, the only fencing close to a road was by the entrance. Did I want to take that chance?

No.

I drove the side roads again. On what I thought to be the backside of the sanctuary, there was nothing but woods. As I parked the car near a small bridge spanning a creek, the adrenaline kicked in. My thought was to hike along the water in search of the fence. I brought the bolt cutters, just in case, tucking them in the back waistband of my pants so they were concealed by my coat. As I made my way through brambles and fallen trees, I came to the realization that this couldn't be a nighttime endeavor. A couple hundred feet in, I found what I was looking for: the fence. It snaked through the woods with a three-foot-wide mowed-clearing along the outside. There were no deer to be seen. Nor any cameras. All was quiet. It was now or never. The hike would be impossible in the dark.

Nervous and jittery, I started snipping the wires. It took about five minutes to clip as high as I could reach and six feet along the top. Peeling the fence back was like opening a gate. I intertwined the cut wires with the stationary fence so it would stay put. I hadn't brought the apples along, and I wasn't going to go back for them. This was it. I prayed the deer found the opening before anyone from Blue Sky noticed it.

I retraced my steps back to the car. Relaxation didn't come until the car started and I was driving away.

The change of plans put me way ahead of schedule. I considered calling Sara to tell her I'd be earlier than expected but decided to do a little shopping instead. I had passed a secondhand store on the drive, and browsing through junk sounded appealing. As I drove, the hat, glasses and wig came off and, once again, I was a woman. In the parking lot of the store, I stuffed the costume into my backpack and removed the jacket.

An older lady greeted me when I entered the store, asking if she could help.

"No, I'm just looking. Needed to stretch my legs," I commented.

"If you have any questions, I'm here."

The shelves were filled with a little bit of everything: musty hardcover books, Tupperware bowls, costume jewelry, knickknacks, iron skillets. The back part of the store was geared toward men and had tables packed with outdated tools, fishing poles, license plates and other manly gear. My heart skipped a beat when I spotted a wooden box of rusted leghold traps. I picked one up and tried to pry the jaws open. The tension was strong, and I didn't want it to snap shut and crush my fingers. The entire box was priced at $20. For that amount, I'd buy them just to ensure they never killed another animal.

"They're for my husband," I told the woman at checkout.

"Did you see the fur?" she asked.

When I said no, she led me to a booth filled with clothes. She removed an item from a rack and held it out to me.

"What is it?" I asked.

"A fox. It was once all the rage for women to wear these over their shoulders," she claimed.

The pelt of the animal was draped around a hanger; it's head, fully intact, rested on its front paws. The eyes stared blankly, and the creature's lifeless tail hung limp.

"Really?" I asked. I didn't share my real feelings with her—that it was wrong for such a majestic animal to be killed for a fashion statement. "How much is it?" I asked, thinking I could lay it to rest next to the fur coat.

"I can let you have it for 10 dollars," she said. "It was 20, but it's been here for months. Not much of a market for these. Today's women want fur coats. What does your husband do with the furs he traps?"

"He doesn't trap, but he hunts. I thought he might like the traps to decorate his trophy room."

"There's not much money in trapping these days. There's more to be made in ranching," she offered.

"What do you mean?"

"The ranchers raise foxes and minks on farms for their fur."

"I didn't know that. Around here?"

"There's a mink farm about an hour north of here."

"So, there's good money to be made? Maybe my husband would be interested," I said, thinking that if a husband of mine hunted or even considered trapping he wouldn't be my husband for very long. "Do you know the name of the place?"

"I can find it for you." I followed her back to the cash register where she disappeared into her office. A few minutes later, she returned and handed me a slip of paper. Written on it was "Fin Fur Farm." She included an address and a telephone number.

I thanked her, paid for my traps and fox pelt and went to the car where I sat in stunned silence. How had the fact escaped me that there were fox and mink farms so close to my home?

Chapter 42

With time to spare before needing to be at Sara's house, I Googled the address of the fox farm, which led me to a satellite view of the operation. The satellite view revealed a house with a swimming pool in the backyard and several roofs of what I guessed to be pole barns. I considered doing a drive-by, but what good would it do? The online imagery exposed more than what could be seen from the road. I needed to learn more about fur farming, and that would be easier done on my computer at home.

On a whim, I went to Amazon on my phone and searched for books about fur farms. A manual on how to raise mink came up, but that wasn't what I wanted. I refined my search by looking for books about animal rights. I choose two: one by Peter Young and the Animal Liberation Front, and another one by Rodney Coronado, who called himself an animal liberation front warrior. Seems I was a little late to the party. People had been freeing animals from injustice for years.

Next stop would be Sara's. The greatest hits of Gordon Lightfoot once again kept me company and diverted my thoughts as I put miles behind me. With the windows rolled down, the autumn air filled my senses with freedom. The distractions didn't hold. The satellite picture of the fox farm invaded my mind. What kinds of horrors were hidden below those roofs? My imagination conjured up rows of small cages housing scared wild animals. Was there nothing people wouldn't do to make a buck?

I called Sara when I was about an hour away from her place and asked if it was okay if I arrived early. She didn't mind.

"You'll be here in time to walk to the lake for the sunset. Will you be up for that?" she asked.

"Sounds perfect after being in the car so long," I replied.

"Then we can come back here for soup. I'm making a veggie stew and baking bread."

"My mouth is watering," I said, thinking to myself that veggie stew was popular this time of year.

Sara lived a few blocks from the state park in Grand Haven. Walking to Lake Michigan and then out to the end of the pier had evolved into a tradition for us. Exercise was a good way to relax after driving.

Sara was sitting in a lawn chair sipping iced tea when I pulled into her driveway. She greeted me at the car with a big hug. Spotting the box of traps topped with the fur in my backseat, she asked what they were for.

"Purchases from a secondhand store. I was ahead of schedule, so I stopped to look around," I explained.

"Why the hell would you buy traps and a fur?"

"I bought the traps to throw away. They won't be used to kill any more innocent animals. I bought the fur because I felt sorry for it," I explained as I opened the car door and grabbed the fox.

"Sorry for it?" Sara questioned.

"Look at it," I said, showing her the pathetic remnants of the once vibrant animal. When she saw the face, she pouted her lips and refused to touch it.

"What the hell is it?" she asked in a horrified voice.

"A vintage fox stole or scarf. Not sure what it's called. It's worn around the neck."

"What are you going to do with it?"

"Bury it."

"Why?"

"To give it a respectable burial."

"Is burial proper for foxes?"

Her question made me stop and think. "I don't know. Maybe not. What should I do with it?"

"I don't know ... return it to the wild? What happens to a fox when it dies naturally?"

"Nature reclaims it?" I guessed.

"Maybe letting it rot in the weather would be more fitting," Sara suggested.

"You're right," I agreed. "I could return it to nature. Leave it down by the river. Let it be free. Let it feel the sun."

Sara started laughing. "It's dead. It's not going to feel the sun."

"I know that. But I'll feel better thinking it does," I acknowledged. Her laughing was contagious, and I laughed, too, as I saw the absurdity in the situation.

"It just looked so forlorn in that store. I couldn't leave it there," I told her as I tried to make her understand why I bought it.

"I get it," she said. "It's ridiculous that women thought wearing these was fashionable."

"But people still wear fur. The heads aren't attached anymore, but every fur was once an animal with a head."

"Let's walk," Sara suggested, "or we'll miss the sunset."

I put the fur back in the car.

"Why so concerned about fur?" Sara asked me as we walked.

She didn't know anything about Buster and Stanley. "It's a long story."

"Well, we have all night," she reminded me.

I gave her the abbreviated version as we walked.

"Oh my God, you were kidnapped?" she shouted. We were on the pier and people were staring at us after her outburst.

I put my finger to my lips to signal her to calm down. "I was, but I'm fine."

"You have to be more careful. You're going to get yourself killed if you keep this up," she reprimanded.

"I *am* careful. I'm okay," I said, trying to reassure her.

At the end of the pier we sat down on the concrete with our backs against the lighthouse. The sun hung above the horizon in a cloudless sky, its fading light softening the last remnants of the day in yellows, reds and darkening blues. Within seconds, it started its descent into the lake and then disappeared.

We shared the spectacular sight with a handful of sunset worshipers who had made the pilgrimage to watch the day slip away. The lights on the pier's catwalk came to life to guide us back to shore. In the twilight, we walked along the beach before cutting back up to the road to walk the asphalt path. Sara, always prepared, had a flashlight.

"I want to hear all the details," she said.

"Give me dinner and a beer and I'll spill my guts," I offered.

Chapter 43

The aroma of fresh baked bread greeted us when we entered the house. Sara's husband, Ryan, had arrived home while we were walking and joined us for dinner before retreating to his office.

"You girls have fun. I have work to do," he said as he gave Sara a kiss.

Being pregnant, Sara wasn't drinking but insisted I have a beer. "To loosen your tongue," she said in jest, but the joke rang true. She knew I talked more when buzzed.

After making ourselves comfy in the living room, she told me to start at the beginning. I tried to protest, but she stopped me short. "We have all night. I want details."

So, I gave her what she wanted. More than an hour's worth of facts, feelings and opinions. She listened and didn't interrupt, didn't ask questions and didn't comment until I finished. I neglected to tell her about any of the illegal activities.

After questioning how I felt, both physically and emotionally, Sara told me how she felt about the incident, and it wasn't positive.

"Why do you keep getting yourself in life-threatening situations? Do you have a death wish? Grams must have been worried sick," she lectured.

"I didn't do it intentionally and, no, I don't have a death wish," I protested, holding out my hand with the engagement ring. "I have plenty to live for."

She squealed and jumped up to give me a hug. "Why didn't you tell me that first?" she shouted. "I'm so happy for you."

We spent the rest of the evening discussing my wedding. While Cooper and I didn't have any plans or even ideas, Sara did. She was like a wedding planner with endless questions and suggestions.

"I think you should get married outside at the farm. If it rains, we can move into the barn. Nothing formal. Did you pick a date? How many people are you thinking of inviting? What about the menu? Alcohol? Do you want a full bar? Music? Dancing? Where are you going for your honeymoon?"

"Good questions. We haven't made any decisions yet," I confessed. "We did discuss eloping. Get married and tell everyone about it afterwards."

"Promise me you won't do that," she blurted in alarm. "Promise me."

"I can't promise anything. It's not just my wedding. I can't make any decisions without talking them over with Cooper first."

"Men don't care about the details," she claimed.

"That's a stereotype. Some do," I argued. "We can come up with ideas, but I can't commit to anything."

By the time we went to bed, Sara had given me plenty to think about. Getting married at the farm topped the list.

Sara's dismissive attitude regarding the fox fur and her reprimand for getting kidnapped made me thankful that I hadn't told her about any of my after-dark activities. She wouldn't understand and, I admit, sometimes I felt confused by it all. For me, the big picture glowed crystal clear. Killing animals for sport or money, although sometimes legal, was morally wrong. While I've never been one with secrets, my moral compass had shifted and, to keep peace, I no longer shared everything with Sara. Cutting fences to free wildlife had erected a fence around me.

In the morning, Ryan made us pecan pancakes with blueberries. Ryan traveled out of state with his job, so spending time with him was a treat.

"Do you guys have a name picked out for the baby?" I asked. Sara told me they opted not to know the gender of the baby before the birth.

"We keep bouncing names around, but nothing has made a basket yet," Ryan, the sports fanatic, stated.

Sara rolled her eyes. "He wants to name the baby after one of his sports heroes. He hasn't convinced me."

"Good luck with that," I offered, directing the comment to Ryan. We both laughed, knowing Sara usually got her way.

The baby shower started at two o'clock. I told Sara I hadn't had time to get a gift so after breakfast we went shopping.

"This is perfect. You can pick out what you want or you can get a gift certificate to shop after the baby's born," I told her.

We went to a store where I picked out a card. She thought shopping after the baby arrived would be a good idea. I wrote her a check so she wouldn't be limited as to where she could shop.

"This is the easy, but practical way out," I said as I signed the card, tucked the check inside it and sealed both in the envelope.

"Now you have to act surprised when you open it," I told her.

"I can do that," she said with a chuckle.

We had lunch at Morning Star Café and then went to the shower. The afternoon was a blur of trying to remember names, playing silly baby games, eating desserts and watching Sara truly get excited at each gift she opened.

Seeing the sleepers, diapers, booties and other baby stuff woke my mothering instinct. The wedding couldn't come fast enough. I wanted a baby-making honeymoon.

I didn't hang around after we got back to Sara's house. I helped unload the gifts, hugged her goodbye and looked forward to a quiet drive back to the farm.

Chapter 44

After spending the afternoon with a house full of boisterous, celebrating women, my soul relished the solitude of the drive home. I didn't even listen to music. My thoughts drifted to my future and to what would make me happy. I loved living on the farm. My best childhood memories came from the summers spent with Grams and Gramps: being outside, helping with the chores, riding horses, pulling weeds in the vegetable garden and swapping stories on the porch in the evenings.

Deciding to stay on the farm was easy. I loved the idea of turning it into a sanctuary, but was it feasible? The peacefulness of SASHA Farm came to mind, a place where farm animals lived out their natural lives without confinement, where kids could visit and meet animals.

Out of the blue, I had an epiphany. We could host summer camps for children and plant the seeds of compassion. The camps would generate an income, and the kids would learn about farm animals. We'd feed the campers a plant-based diet, and they'd discover that healthy nutrition didn't have to include killing cows, pigs, chickens or any other animal.

The farm could also be a nonprofit so we could seek donations. With the internet and social media, finding like-minded people who would support the venture would be easy.

By the time I got home, my mind brimmed with ideas and excitement. I shared them with Grams as we sat on the porch swing, my enthusiasm contagious.

"I love the idea," she said. "There's a ton of details to work out, but I bet we could get it together to have our first campers next summer."

I grabbed a notebook and, as we brainstormed, took notes that included a to-do list: look into becoming a nonprofit, check on insurance for a sanctuary and insurance for having campers, how much should we charge kids to come to our camp, where would the kids sleep?

"I would love a bunkhouse," I told Grams. "I can see a building with a room for boys and another one for girls. There would be bunkbeds. We'd need bathrooms and showers, a kitchen and dining hall. What kind of activities? How many at a time?"

One question led to another. It didn't take long to become overwhelmed.

"Do you want something to drink? A glass of wine?" I asked.

"I'll get it, you keep writing," she suggested as she headed inside.

She returned with two glasses of merlot. It softened my thinking as we discussed what we should work on first.

"Probably the nonprofit paperwork. I've heard it's a lengthy process and takes time," Grams said. "Looking at the cost of insurance is probably important. We need to figure out all the expenses before we can set a price."

"We could start small to see how it goes. Have the kids stay in the house or a tent. If it goes well, we could get a loan and build a bunkhouse. We could even have a couple cottages for families to visit," I said before realizing I was getting carried away. "That could be phase two."

"I like the idea of starting small," Grams said.

"I do too," I agreed.

Just before heading upstairs for the night, Grams told me a package had been delivered for me.

"My books," I said when I saw the Amazon packaging. Grabbing the package, I went to my bedroom and cut the tape on the box as I called Cooper. I was eager to share with him the ideas for the farm.

He listened as my excitement dominated the conversation. When I exhausted my enthusiasm, he finally had a chance to speak. He said he liked the plan of having a summer camp for children. "Your past led you to this," he said.

"You think?" I asked.

He knew I cherished my memories of spending summers on the farm as a kid and how much I loved the opportunity to live there with Grams. Plus, I had been a grade-school teacher. When my son became sick, my teaching days had come to a screeching halt.

"You like kids, and your teaching background will certainly give you credibility," he added.

We talked for more than an hour about the future. I told him Sara suggested we have our wedding on the farm. "Something small," I said.

"Whatever you want, but the smaller the better," he said.

"Now we just need to figure out when. What do you think of the fall, a year from now?" I asked.

"I'm still trying to find out when I can move to Michigan. As soon as I know that, we can figure out a date. Or we can get married and not live together. I would suggest you move here, but I know better than to even ask that."

As much as I enjoyed my visit to California, I much preferred Michigan. I couldn't leave Grams either.

After our talk, I turned my attention to my new books. I started reading *Flaming Arrows* and stayed up another two hours with my attention hooked on the stories.

Needless to say, I slept late Sunday morning. When I went downstairs, Grams was reading the paper and drinking coffee.

"Look at this," she said, sliding the paper across the table.

My picture graced the front page, the same one of me dressed as Al that had been in the paper before. Next to it were photographs of cut fences. The accompanying article took up half the front page and jumped to the inside.

"Are you involved?" she asked.

I ignored her as I read. Fences had been cut at several canned-hunting facilities across the state. Police thought it was the work of more than one person, perhaps copycats that were inspired by the original article, which had been published in several papers statewide.

"Did you read it?" I asked. "It says they suspect copycats. I haven't been traveling all over the state so they must be copycats."

"Is Cooper involved? Did you really go to the U.P. or were you up to no good?"

"We were in the U.P." I grabbed my phone and clicked on photos. "Here's proof. Look at the photos." She scrolled though the snapshots. "Believe me now?" I asked, getting irritated that she didn't believe me or maybe because she was right, and I was deceitful.

"Yes, but when I read that article it sure sounded like something the two of you would do."

I laughed. "You're right. If I had thought of it, I probably would have. But I can tell you this—Cooper never would have. He's been in prison and will never go back."

"Good. Glad he has a brain."

I read the article again. "I'm thrilled that I motivated someone else to take action," I confessed.

But I was also worried. A $10,000 reward was being offered for any leads to the identity of the person in the photo or to find who was involved in the damages.

Chapter 45

Driving to work gave me a sense of normalcy, which I appreciated. Walking in, I had a flash of déjà vu. Just like the previous Monday, Cindi, Jason and Carol were sitting in the breakroom. Cindi had picked up donuts again to celebrate my return.

"Welcome back," she said, giving me a hug.

Next, Carol embraced me. "I'm so thankful you're okay," she whispered.

I thanked her and assured her that I was fine.

"Didn't we celebrate my return last Monday?" I joked.

"Like I said before, we look for any excuse to have donuts," Jason acknowledged.

I laughed and sat down. Cindi poured me a cup of coffee, and Jason set down a plate with an apple fritter in front of me. Again, déjà vu.

It's good to be back ... again," I said, raising my coffee cup. They followed my lead, and we clinked our mugs together.

"A full crew," Cindi said. "Let's hope it lasts a little longer than a few hours."

"I'm not going anywhere," I said. "And if I do, I'll take Jason with me. I learned my lesson." They all chuckled. "What? You don't believe me?"

"We know you better than that," Cindi replied. "I'm sure you mean it today. But tomorrow? I'm betting you'll forget."

"I have to agree with Cindi," Jason said. "I'll put my money on you forgetting the minute you see an animal who needs to be rescued."

"I think I learned my lesson this time. I really thought I was going to die ... and I don't want to die."

Carol started crying and grabbed my arm. "Just don't take any more chances. Take Jason with you next time. He's got a gun."

I patted her hand. "I'll be careful," I assured her. "And I'll take Jason."

"Good. Glad we have that settled," Jason said. "Seriously, call me. I'm always available when you need me."

Their expressions of concern and caring made my eyes brim with love.

"Thank you," I whispered. "Thank you. Your concern means the world to me."

Our conversation switched to our Monday morning staff meeting. Cindi filled me in on the residents who had been adopted and of the newcomers. Carol talked about her work with farmers and convincing them to get their barn cats spayed and neutered. Jason reported on Stanley, saying the case was closed, as was case of Joe DeYoung who Stanley murdered.

After we finished, Jason asked if he could talk to me privately in my office.

"Sure. What's up?" I asked.

He didn't answer until after he closed the door and we were alone. He pulled a newspaper from his clipboard and handed it to me. "Tell me this isn't you."

It was the front page of Sunday's paper.

"You think that's me? I read it yesterday. I can only wish I had the guts to do such a thing," I said, trying to remain calm, despite my heart pounding so loudly I was sure Jason could hear it.

"You didn't answer my question. The getup looks a lot like what you wore to the dogfight. Is it you?"

"No, it isn't me," I said, staring directly into Jason's eyes. I hated to lie, but Jason, besides being a friend, was a county deputy. I couldn't tell him the truth.

He hesitated a few seconds before responding causing me mental turmoil. *What did he know?*

"I'll take your word, but let me warn you, Alison. Be careful. They're increasing their security. They want to catch whoever is doing this and make them an example. When they do—and believe me they will—whoever it is will be doing some serious time."

"It's not me," I protested, my voice rising in anger. "And I don't know anything about it."

"Good," he replied.

Jason left, but I didn't think he believed me. I went through the day worrying that he might search the house but came to the conclusion that Jason wanted to believe me and, as long as I didn't give him any more reasons not to, he would let it be.

That night after dinner, I took Dappy for a ride. On the bank of the river, as tears streamed down my face, I buried my wig, glasses and the jacket in a deep grave. Along with them, I buried my dream of liberating every animal from the chains and cages of inhumanity. I marked the grave with the fox fur. I could hear Sara say, *It's dead. It's not going to feel the sun.*

I knew she was right, but returning the fur to nature felt good. Perhaps its spirit would feel the freedom, soak in the warmth of the sun, trot through the woods by the light of the moon, feel the gentleness of summer rain, inhale the sweet scent of the pine and hear the rustle of the oak leaves.

"I'm sorry I can't do more," I said as tears stained my face. "I'm so sorry."

Chapter 46

The feeling of defeat stayed with me throughout the night. At work the next day, Cindi knocked on my office door and asked if I could help with a surrendered pig.

"Pig? Did I hear you right? Someone is surrendering a pig?" I asked.

"It's a first," she said rolling her eyes.

In the lobby, a woman held a medium-size dog carrier that held a pig squealing in distress. The woman shook my hand and told me her name was Rose. After introducing myself, I asked her why she wanted us to take the pig.

"It's a Juliana pig," she said.

"A what?"

"It's a breed of miniature pig. I thought I could handle her, but she's like a two-year-old kid—stubborn and obstinate. I now know where the term pigheaded comes from. I can't take it anymore," Rose told me with tears in her eyes.

"I don't have any experience with pigs," I admitted. "Is she mean? If we let her out, will we be in trouble?"

"No, as long as you have a box of these you'll be in control. Jules loves them," Rose said drying her tears and handing me a baggie filled with something. "Cheerios. She loves them."

"Let's go to my office," I suggested.

Rose followed with the carrier and the squealing Jules.

In my office, I closed the door and sat on the floor with the carrier in front of me. Slowly I opened its door. A black snout became visible.

"Jules," Rose called.

I fell in love the instant I saw Jules. She was the size of a two-liter bottle of soda and had a gray coat sprinkled with black spots.

Rose threw a handful of cereal on the floor. Jules trotted over to the morsels and sucked them up like a vacuum cleaner, all the time her tiny tail twirled in happiness.

"She's so small," I said with delight. "And so cute. How can you give her up?"

"She's demanding. She needs training like a dog, and I don't have what it takes," she responded. "I love her dearly, but I just can't keep her."

I recognized Jules as a sign that starting a farm sanctuary was the right thing to do. I shared with Rose my dream of a teaching sanctuary and told her I'd be interested in adopting Jules. She loved the idea and even offered to help.

Jules pointed my life in what I knew was the right direction. My future looked promising, and I was excited about it. Cooper, the wedding, and starting a sanctuary and a family.

As Cindi and I said goodbye to Rose, a floral delivery woman walked into the shelter.

"Is there an Alison Cavera here?" the young woman asked.

Cindi pointed to me.

"These are for you," she said, handing me a cellophane-covered flower arrangement.

"What did you do to deserve those?" Cindi asked.

"I don't know," I answered with all honesty. I set the flowers on the counter and carefully removed the protective covering.

"Ohhh, pretty," Cindi fussed as a dozen roses—five red and seven white—were revealed.

I read the attached card. "Welcome to the Save Five Club, Love, Cooper." I slipped the card into my pocket, not wanting to answer questions about the club.

"They're from Cooper," I told them, smiling.

Remembering My Friend
No mushrooms, no green peppers

Scrawled on the Christmas card from Wendy was, "I have big news. I'll call you after the holidays."

I first met Wendy Wamser in the 1980s. After becoming a vegetarian, I joined West Michigan for Animals where she was already a member. The group broke up about ten years later, but our friendship remained.

Wendy was an animal rights activist. Among other activities, she picketed rodeos, circuses, research labs that used animals and any other business that used and abused animals.

I can't remember the exact year, but sometime in the mid 1990s I had the brilliant idea to organize a kayaking birthday party for myself. I called girlfriends, sisters and nieces. On a whim, we decided to have a potluck afterwards and since it was my birthday and I was vegetarian, everyone had to bring a non-meat dish to share. Wendy loved the idea because she didn't eat meat either. She also didn't eat eggs or dairy. Plus, she hated mushrooms and green peppers. She could sniff out a mushroom from five feet away and spot a pepper no matter how well disguised.

That first kayaking party was so enjoyable that it became an annual event. Sometimes they were adventures. Like the time I spotted a paddle and kayak floating down the river. Who was missing? Wendy. She had been indecisive on which side of an island she wanted to paddle around. By not deciding, she rammed straight into the island and tipped. We found her wading in the mud looking for a lost shoe, which she never found. Another time a ten percent chance of rain turned into an all day rain, we were drenched and cold the entire trip.

The only people, beside myself, who never missed a kayaking trip were my sister, Rose, and Wendy.

After I read the note in Wendy's card, I decided I wasn't going to wait until after the holidays to find out Wendy's big news. I picked up the phone and dialed her number. I told her I couldn't wait.

"What's the big news?"

The first clue something was wrong was when she said she didn't want to ruin my holidays.

"What is it?" I asked.

"You're assuming big news is good news," she said.

That was the second clue.

"You're right. I expected good news. What is it. Tell me."

Janet Vormittag, 4th from left, and Wendy Wamser, 2nd from right.

"I have Stage Four cancer."

She was right. She ruined my holidays.

Wendy told me she wanted to read my next book before she died. I asked her how long I had to write it---at that point the third installment of my series was only percolating in my head.

"Start writing," she ordered. She had only been given a five percent chance of survival.

So I started writing, but I'm a slow writer and the cancer was aggressive. It grew faster than I could put story to paper.

Surgery wasn't an option. Wendy underwent radiation and then chemo. The first round of chemo left her so sick she ended up in the hospital. Three weeks later after the second round, she didn't fare much better. But after the initial sickness caused by the poison injected into her body, she felt much better, declaring she thought the chemo was working. She was making plans for the future. She told me she would have to wear her life jacket when we went kayaking because if she fell in she wouldn't have the strength to swim. I told her that would be a great idea. Drowning wouldn't make for a good adventure.

Her hopes of the chemo working were dashed after more tests and the doctor's grim report that the cancer was still growing. There would be no more treatment. Only pain pills.

Wendy died Friday, May 31, 2019 with two friends, her dog and three cats by her side.

She passed three weeks before our kayaking trip.

Wendy will be with me whenever I'm kayaking or eating mushrooms or green peppers. Instead of her reading *The Save Five Club*, it is dedicated to her.

About the Author

Janet Vormittag uses her writing to advocate for animals. She is the founder and publisher of *Cats and Dogs, a Magazine Devoted to Companion Animals*, which is distributed in West Michigan. She has a bachelor's degree in journalism from Grand Valley State University and was a correspondent for *The Grand Rapids Press* for ten years.

www.janetvormittag.com